# BARRON'S BRIDE

## SEVEN BRIDES FOR SEVEN BROTHERS
### BOOK SIX

## KATHLEEN LAWLESS

ISBN ebook: 978-1-9990635-2-8

ISBN print: 978-1-989873-53-3

### *Seven Brides for Seven Brothers* **Reviews**

What reviewers are saying about the *Seven Brides for Seven Brothers* series...

"GREAT SERIES!!!" Top 500 reviewer

"If you have not picked up the series, do yourself a favor, you will be glad you do."

"I loved the continuity in the series—and the resolution"

"Sweet and romantic."

"This entire series is going into my library to be read again and again."

"I just love reading Kathleen's books—they keep me coming back for more."

If you haven't already done so, sign up for my VIP Reader's Newsletter and be the first to hear about free books, fan-priced sales, and my new series. Details at the end of the book.

## Dedication

Dedicated to all my readers who are embracing this series.
Thank you!

# CHAPTER 1

L ily stood next to her sister, Rose, and listened with half an ear as the reverend recited the words that would bind Rose and Bishop to each other until death. Bride and groom looked deeply and soulfully into each other's eyes as they repeated their vows. On the other side of Bishop Lily saw Barron, Bishop's twin, watching her, his eyes narrowed. Lily looked past him as if he didn't exist.

Today was a day of celebration, the type of gathering of family members and loved ones that she had never been part of before. Such a shame that Barron had to be here to ruin it.

BARRON KNEW he should be used to weddings by now. The suit that he'd bought last year for Brody's big day was nearly worn out from all the weddings that followed. So why did he feel so uneasy standing here next to Bishop, listening to his twin pledge himself to Rose till death? Sounded like one heck of a long time to him.

Since the day they were born it had been him and Bishop, united against the world. Was he jealous? Feeling his place in his brother's life usurped by a woman?

He'd been surprised to learn the wedding would take place here at the Copper Moon Ranch; the place was a working ranch where the brothers all lived with their brides. He and Ben were the only two sane ones, the bachelors of the group. Still, the old place looked good, all decked out by the ladies with flowers and fancy ribbons on the makeshift platform he'd helped build for the ceremony. Afterward it would double as a dance floor.

He glanced again at Rose's sister, Lily. There was definitely something about her that he didn't trust. Maybe now that her sister was married, Lily would up and leave town. Be a good thing for everyone here if she high-tailed it back to Yuma, or better yet, some place far, far away. He knew, sure as he drew his next breath, that if Lily stuck around, she was going to raise havoc in all their lives.

The ceremony didn't last long, but in his world, it seemed to drag on forever. He could barely stomach the sight of Lily standing there next to the bride, looking as if butter wouldn't melt in her sweet little mouth.

He didn't buy any part of her story except the part where she'd been kidnapped, and only because Rose had seen the whole thing. When he and Bishop found her, Lily pretended she'd lost her memory along with her ability to speak. Pretended to not even know her own sister. Convenient how her memory returned in a hurry when it suited her.

He had a feeling things were all about whether or not they suited Lily. He'd seen red the night he'd witnessed her talking to that goon of Hawkes's. It had been a pleasure to shoot the guy while pretending to be defending Lily. Lily

2

claimed he'd been the same man who'd kidnapped her. Shame Barron hadn't minded his own business. Let the vermin take Lily away again. Except Rose would be back on Bishop and him to go find her again. Playing the role of Lily's savior once was enough.

He started when he felt his arm pinched, bringing him back to the present. Lily stood next to him, practically on top of him. "The ceremony is over, in case you hadn't noticed. This is where you take my arm and we follow the bride and groom down into the yard."

"Right," he said with a near growl. Just his luck to be best man to Lily's maid of honor. As if the woman before him had any sense of honor.

Not that he was exactly anyone's idea of a "best man." Not given some of the things he'd seen and done. The wedding had thrown them together a lot recently, what with rehearsals and all that nonsense. Thank goodness the entire ordeal was nearly over.

He gritted his teeth as Lily tucked her arm against his.

"The receiving line will be over here. In case you weren't paying attention the other day."

Barron's breath hissed between his teeth. Why did the woman irritate him so much every time she opened her mouth? "I was paying attention. It's not exactly my first time at the rodeo, you know."

Lily responded with a disdainful sniff.

When they had taken their places in line, she said, "I hope you have your speech all prepared. I'd hate to see you make more of a fool of yourself than usual."

He ground his teeth together and clamped his lips tightly shut, afraid of what he might say if he opened his mouth.

Lily hadn't been in town long, yet somehow she

managed to remember everyone's name better than he did, as the townsfolk shuffled through the line to offer up their congratulations to the newlyweds.

"How'd you do that?" he asked at one point, when she addressed by name not only a rancher that Barron knew only on sight, but the names of his wife and four children as well.

"I care about people," she said simply. "Unlike you, who only cares about himself."

"I protected you from getting snatched up by Hawkes's goon at that Halloween party."

"Truth is, you shot him because he was one of Hawkes's men. My being there just gave you a handy excuse."

Over his dead body would Barron admit she was right. He had thought she was teaming up with the other side. Which he still suspected, given as nothing he saw or heard since had convinced him otherwise. For a certainty, the insufferable Miss Lily bore watching.

At last the glad-handing was over.

"Where are you going?" she asked.

"Taking a turn with the others to keep an eye out for intruders."

"Intruders? At a wedding?"

"Hawkes has busted up a few weddings now. Along with Charlotte's christening. Something about us all being together sees him hell-bent on inflicting pain and suffering."

"I hate bullies." Lily spoke with a vehemence that surprised him.

"Hawkes is the biggest bully you'll ever be unfortunate enough to set eyes on."

"Hah! And here I thought that title belonged to you, Barron Mason." Insult delivered, she turned on her heel and made her way across the ranch yard to where the other women were gathered.

"IS BARRON OFF TO KEEP WATCH?" Storm, one of the Mason brides, asked.

Lily nodded. "He said Hawkes enjoys disrupting things."

Storm nodded. "Hawkes set a cache of dynamite not far from Braydon and Henrietta's wedding in the park. Blake risked his life to throw the entire thing in the river." She smiled a secret smile. "He was so brave. I swear I fell in love with him right then and there."

Lily took a second look at Storm's husband, the quietest of the seven brothers. Nothing about his demeanor screamed "hero". But as she saw Storm's nod in response to a silent message passed between him and Storm, she guessed he was also off to keep an eye out for intruders.

"Are you planning to stay here in town, Lily?" Storm asked. "Now that the wedding is over and your sister is settled."

"I'm not really sure."

Ever since day one, it had been her and Rose together. Even after she was kidnapped, she'd had no doubt Rose would hunt her down to the ends of the earth. They had always been there watching out for each other. It was going to be quite an adjustment, her sister as a married woman.

"Poor Barron seems a bit lost," Storm said. "This will be a big change for him. The way I understand it, the twins have been nearly inseparable their entire lives."

"Uh, huh." Lily hoped nothing she said or did would elicit similar words of sympathy. After all, she was her own woman for the first time ever. Something she was looking forward to.

"Barron must be nervous about his upcoming speech toasting the happy couple, because he asked me to read it over," Storm said. "I made a few changes."

Lily nodded. Bishop asking Storm for help made sense, seeing as how Storm was a librarian and the one who taught Blake how to read. "Are you planning to take the mobile library around soon?"

"That depends," Storm said. "Blake doesn't want me going off alone, and he's reluctant to leave the ranch these days. All the boys are expecting another move from Hawkes."

"Rose said she really enjoyed it when she went off in the book-lending wagon with the twins," Lily said.

Storm did a double take. "Rose went out in the book-lending wagon?"

"It was when the twins were helping her look for me. I didn't know you didn't know about it."

"She's been helping me in the library we set up at the new Women's Institute Hall. I guess that explains how she caught on so fast. Trust the twins to keep it a secret."

"Maybe I shouldn't have told you," Lily said.

"You'd think I'd be used to it by now. This family and their penchant for keeping secrets." Storm gave a short laugh. "Not that I'm one to talk. Oops, Henrietta is flagging me down."

She turned and hastened off before Lily could ask what she meant about the family and its secrets. When Lily glanced down, she saw a folded piece of paper. Storm must have dropped it on the ground.

She swooped down to pick it up and quickly unfolded it. Barron's speech! She tucked it in her bosom, then turned and sauntered in the opposite direction.

HALFWAY DOWN THE ranch's driveway Barron ran into Benjamin. The two men exchanged a look.

"Be nice to get things back to normal around here," Benjamin said. He had a rifle in one hand and a pistol on his belt, quite at odds with the groomsmen suits they all wore.

"Amen to that," Barron said. He tugged on his lapels. "I'll be happy to retire this and get back into some real clothes." He looked back to where the wedding guests milled about near the big ranch house. "Think we can stay out here till after Bishop tosses the bride's garter?"

"I'm all for that," Benjamin agreed. He and Barron shared a smile remembering how Bishop had caught the garter at the last wedding, just before Rose had caught the bouquet. Not that Barron was superstitious or anything, but no point tempting fate.

He was glad to have Benjamin at his side as they strolled the length of the driveway in companionable silence, eyes on the surrounding undergrowth for signs of furtive movement or anything out of place. The Copper Moon Ranch sat on a huge parcel of land that had originally belonged to Brody's uncle and was impossible to fully secure, especially after Hawkes bought the ranch next door.

"Have you seen anything interesting going on near Hawkes's lately?" Benjamin asked as they turned around and slowly headed back toward the festivities.

Barron shook his head. Benjamin knew about the secret spot Barron and Bishop had carved out to keep an eye on Hawkes from a distance whenever they could.

All too soon, it seemed, they ended up back in the thick of the wedding festivities. "Another run?" Barron asked, hoping to delay the inevitable— taking his seat at the head table close to Lily.

Benjamin wasn't fooled. "Aren't you supposed to be giving a speech soon?"

"Right," Barron said. "I'd better go find Storm. I left it with her."

He wove through the guests, some of whom mistook him for Bishop and stopped him, offering up their congratulations. Times past, he and Bishop would make a game out of fooling folks, pretending to be each other, but today of all days he wasn't interested in playing.

Eventually he intercepted Storm as she ran between the ranch house kitchen and the food table, a steaming casserole dish in her hands. "I figured I'd better get my speech off you," he said.

"Sure thing. Just let me put this down first."

He had to admit the ranch looked good, all dusted off and clad in her best finery for the occasion. Visible on the slight rise behind the ranch house and the barn, with a view of the Colorado River, stood five recently built cabins, one for each newlywed couple to call home and carve out some privacy. Soon as they lost the sun later today, there would be lanterns and candles galore to keep the party going.

Storm put down her serving dish and reached into the side pocket of her gown. Her eyes widened as she pulled out her hand and checked the other pocket. "That's odd. It's not here."

Barron looked at the food table. "Did you lay it down someplace? Inside maybe?"

Storm shook her head. "I wanted it close at hand

because I didn't know when I would see you to give it to you."

Barron tried not to panic. "It has to be here someplace. Maybe you dropped it."

"I was talking to Lily after the ceremony. I'll go find her and see if maybe I dropped it and she picked it up."

"Never mind," Barron said. "You've got stuff here to see to. I'll go find her."

Before seeking out Lily, he did a good hunt around the yard and grounds among the guests, hoping against hope he'd spot a folded piece of white paper lying unnoticed in the dust.

LILY SAW BARRON'S SHORT, intense conversation with Storm, followed by his close scrutiny of the area.

It felt good knowing she had the power to make him squirm and sweat a little longer, and that she could put him out of his misery whenever she chose. She was just about to take pity on him when he strode toward her, a belligerent scowl on his face.

"I suppose you're enjoying this," he said.

Lily blinked innocently. "Enjoying what?"

"You know exactly what's going on. Don't bother pretending that you don't."

"Sorry, I don't do word puzzles." She turned her back, any glimmer of sympathy washed away by his accusations. True accusations, mind you, but it wouldn't hurt him to be more gracious. After all, she had something he wanted.

His grip on her forearm prevented her from leaving. "I haven't trusted you since I first laid eyes on you at Zara's. You and your dumb mute act."

"And I'm tired of your accusations. You think I'm some sort of spy for Hawkes, a man I've never even laid eyes on. A man whose name I never heard until you and your brother corralled me to this one-horse town."

"We brought you here for your sister's sake, not yours," he said. "You're free to leave anytime."

"You'd like that, wouldn't you!" She reached into her décolletage with her free hand and pulled out the paper. "You'll be needing this. I was on my way to give it to you when you came stomping over throwing around falsehoods." She gave her arm a shake to try and free it from his grip. "Can I go now?"

Barron released her and snatched the paper from her hand in one swift blur of movement.

"You're welcome," she said sarcastically. "Seeing as how I saved it from getting ground into the dirt." She half turned away, before she flung her parting remark. "Bully!"

"Wait!"

Reluctantly, she turned back.

"I'm sorry," he mumbled.

She stepped closer. "What was that? I'm afraid I didn't hear you very clearly on account of all the noise of the wedding."

Barron eyes bored into hers. "I said I was sorry."

"For what?" she said. "Bullying me? Or misjudging and mistrusting me since we met?"

His body language—clenched fists and tense shoulders—clearly said he didn't like being cornered. "You can accept my apology or not. Up to you."

She gave him a light pat on his forearm. "Better get used to practicing your 'sorries.' I have a feeling you're going to need them."

Lily left Barron with his mouth hanging open. Today

was Rose's day, and she wasn't about to let some loud-mouth bully ruin it.

The crowd around the bride had thinned out by the time she made her way to her sister's side. The two exchanged a secret look the way they had when they were younger. Given all the times their father had set their penance for imagined sin at silence, they had learned to communicate with a look or a gesture.

"You look so happy," she told Rose.

"I am. Whoever would have thought, living out of the back of the preaching wagon, that we could somehow find our way to a place like this? A life that's normal. Folks who are genuinely nice."

In spite of herself, Lily sighed. "Normal. I like the sound of that."

"And you like the Masons, right?" Rose asked anxiously. "Because you know, my new family will always be your family."

"I like most of them," Lily said carefully. "The wives, especially, are all lovely women."

"Yes," Rose said. "None of them are anyone's doormat."

They were both silent for a second, thinking about their mother.

"Do you wish ma was here today?" Lily asked.

Rose shook her head. "This is a new chapter in my life. She never understood us. She would never understand this life or why we like it here so much." She changed the subject abruptly. "What are you going to do next?"

Lily puffed out a thoughtful breath. "We saw a lot of wrong being done when we were growing up. Pa bullying and forcing people to see and do things his way. I know I can't do much on my own, but I'd like to somehow make a difference. Make bad things better any way I can."

Her plan had been forming for a while now, but wasn't ready to share. Since arriving she'd heard the stories of how Hawkes had tried to kill Laura, confined and beaten Bradley, burned down Amanda's family home and committed other innumerable affronts against the Mason clan. Her father had also attacked people, just in different ways, claiming to be doing the work of God.

She hadn't been able to stop her father, but maybe she could do something about Hawkes. Even though she and Hawkes had never laid eyes on each other, the hatred she bore her father had found a new target.

She didn't miss the scrutinizing look Rose leveled her way. "I haven't seen this crusader side of you before."

"I believe it's something new I discovered since getting away from our parents."

ROSE WATCH HER SISTER CLOSELY. "You're worrying me, Lily."

Lily leaned forward and pressed a kiss to her brow. "No bride is allowed to be worried on her wedding day." She gave Rose a little push. "Go be with your new husband. Everything with me is just fine."

Rose reached Bishop's side and instantly relaxed as she felt his arm around her.

"No love lost between your sister and Barron, is there?" he said.

"Why do you say that?"

"You haven't seen the two of them throwing daggers at each other when they're in close proximity."

Rose turned to her new husband. "I'm sure you're imagining things. Lily is just adjusting to life here, is all."

"So why the worried frown when you two were talking just now?"

She glanced up at him. Word was, secrets ran rampant through the Mason clan, but she didn't want to start married life with anything less than honesty between them. "Just something Lily said. About righting the world's wrongs."

Bishop laughed. "It's just talk, my love. What do you bet Lily is feeling a little bit lost? Her life has changed, same as yours." He pointed to where his twin stood talking to Benjamin. "I suspect Barron might be feeling similarly displaced. He and I used to do everything together."

"Even visit the whore houses, I heard," Rose said.

"Who told you that?" Bishop said.

She tapped his chest with her finger. "Just remember, Mr. Mason, I have my sources, same as you."

"Yes, Mrs. Mason."

She smiled at the sound of her new name, then glanced over to where Georgina was beckoning from near the buffet table. "I see Georgina sending us a cue to start things off."

"TALK AROUND TOWN is there's another of them Mason weddings going on over at the ranch," Hawkes said.

"True talk," Denim said. "Me and a few of the others went in for a closer look. Without them catching sight of us, of course."

"Did you find their weak point?"

Denim shook his head.

"Why not?" Hawkes roared.

"Cause they ain't got one," Denim said. "They got groups patrolling any and every spot a man or a horse could make its way in."

"Are you telling me the Copper Moon is impenetrable?"

"I'm telling you today it is. Tomorrow could be a whole different story."

"And if I order you to breach their fortress?"

"Don't mean no offense, boss. But you sent Haywire to go get that little gal and he ended up getting shot dead. None of us around here feels like meeting the same fate."

"You blame me for Haywire getting shot?" Hawkes asked in his lowest, most threatening voice. "You know, same as me, he was killed by one of them Masons."

"Just the same." Denim swallowed thickly. "Gives us good cause to steer them a wide berth. Especially when they got their guard up, like today."

"You didn't used to be such a chicken shit, Denim. Time was you enjoyed killing the same or more than me."

"That ain't changed none. I'm just kind of partial to getting away in one piece, if you catch my drift."

"You don't want to see your usefulness come to an end like poor old Sheriff Yates, now do you?" Hawkes said.

"Never did hear what happened to Yates," Denim said.

"And you never will."

# CHAPTER 2

Barron waited until the rest of the wedding party had filled their plates and taken their seats at the head table before making his way to where the food was laid out. "Looks good," he said as he passed Georgina, who was keeping an eagle eye on the food table as if it was her first-born child.

"I couldn't do all this by myself," she said modestly. She lowered her voice. "Did Lily say anything to you about whether or not she's planning to stay on in Bullet?"

"Why would she tell me?"

"She probably knows you better than anyone else here other than her sister."

Barron didn't care for the sound of that. "I don't think that she and I really—"

*Really what?* See eye-to-eye? Barely tolerate the sight of each other?

"I get the sense Lily feels Bullet doesn't have much to offer her, especially now that Rose is married."

"She's right about that." Barron helped himself to a roll

and a scoop of potato salad. "Best for everyone if she just moves along."

"This town is not for everyone," Georgina agreed.

"You've been here a long time," Barron said.

"Long as anyone else here. At least it sure feels that way."

"Do you remember what town was like before Hawkes came on the scene?"

She forced a laugh. "I'm not that old."

"No," he said. "I guess you're not."

"Anyway, Hawkes is no longer welcome anywhere in town."

Barron looked up. "Since when has that stopped the vermin from showing up wherever he pleases?"

Georgina leaned over and straightened a dish that didn't need straightening. "Today is a happy day. Let's not ruin it by talking about him."

Barron nodded. Unfortunately, nothing ever stopped him from thinking about Hawkes. Anticipating seeing the scumbag dead.

He delivered his wedding toast without a single fumble and breathed a sigh of relief once it was over. Only one more duty to suffer through today and he was free.

On cue, the music started up, signaling the bride and groom's first dance together as a married couple. Followed by the moment he had been dreading. With no parents of the bride or groom to join the newlyweds on the dance floor, he and Lily had been elected to do the honors.

"We're up," he said curtly, pulling back her chair so she could rise more easily.

"Nice scowl." She rose and placed her hand in his so he could lead her to the dancing area. Her hand felt slim and soft against his work-toughened calluses. He'd bet she'd never done a lick of physical labor in her life.

"I'm not scowling," he said. "Just not used to wearing a tie."

"And not really used to dancing, it would seem," she said when he clutched her awkwardly and trod on her foot.

"I tried to beg off," he said. "Bishop insisted."

"And you'd do anything for your brother," she said. "Same as I would for my sister."

He grunted. Last thing he wanted was to have anything in common with the woman he was currently partnered with. The other last thing he wanted was the small surge of awareness at how natural it felt to hold her.

Light on her feet, she easily followed his clumsy lead, fluid in his arms as they found a rhythm that saved her feet and spared his embarrassment. She smelled good too. Something flowery and sweet wafted up from the top of her head to tease his nostrils. Her waist was so small, he could easily span it with his two hands. Not that he was about to try.

He'd been close to her before, he reminded himself. Notably the time they'd shared a mount for most of the return trip from her parents' camp. She'd gone from meek and quiet to a mouthy fireball so fast he hadn't been able to keep up. Even now, he never quite knew who he was going to be faced with when their paths crossed.

Right now, she had her face tilted toward his, studying him closely, making him glad she wasn't able to read his thoughts, which were not up for scrutiny.

"Just so you know, I don't like you any better than you like me," she said.

"No," he said sarcastically. "I never would have guessed."

"I hide it well," she said with that smug smile he was growing to dislike intensely.

He let out a snort. "Good thing we won't be thrown together after today."

"Good thing."

Abruptly he grew aware of the funny looks coming their way and realized the music had stopped. They were the only ones still on the dance floor.

"I bet you're glad that's over." Lily slipped from his arms and left him standing there alone. Mercifully, the musicians started a new song and folks flooded the dance area, allowing him to retreat mostly unnoticed.

Some distance from the dancing and food he spotted Benjamin standing with his back toward him. Another sane bachelor to commiserate with. Except as he drew within earshot, he realized Ben wasn't alone. He was talking to a woman who was sheltered from view by Ben's broad silhouette.

"Don't tell me there's fixing to be another wedding," he muttered to himself as he turned in the opposite direction. He did such an abrupt about face he nearly ran into Bradley and his son.

Barron blinked. He still hadn't gotten used to the sight of Brody or Bradley packing a baby.

"Hey!" he said, not quite knowing what else to say. Bradley wore the same happy grin he'd had ever since he and Amanda got things between them sorted out.

Bradley indicated the sleeping infant. "Sam got a bit fussy when Amanda was trying to enjoy her meal. Soon as I started walking him he settled right down."

Barron ran a hand through his hair. "That's, uh, that's great. Good for you." He struggled for something, anything to add, but what did he know about babies?

"Guess it's a bit of a surprise, your brother getting hitched so sudden- like," Bradley said.

"Bishop said there was no point in waiting. I guess he's right on that count. Unless he wanted to play it smart and wait till Hawkes is well and truly out of the way for good."

Bradley nodded. "That'll happen when the time's right."

Barron swallowed his cynicism. "Sure it will. It's only been— how many years?"

Bradley gave him a knowing look. "We made a pact together, the seven of us that night."

"So Brody keeps reminding me," Barron said. "Like I'm the only one who's running out of patience."

"You're not alone in that," Bradley said. "But Brody worries your fuse might be a little shorter than what the rest of us have."

"What's that supposed to mean?"

"You always did go after a fight," Bradley said.

"Is that what everyone thinks of me? A fighter with a hot temper and a short fuse?"

"Would we be far off?"

Barron fell silent. Seemed he'd been having to fight so long it was all he knew. "Someone around here has to get their hands dirty. Do what needs to be done. We can't all be playing daddy and folding nappies."

Bradley's look was long and level. "That chip on your shoulder getting a little heavy these days?"

Barron opened his mouth to deny having a chip on his shoulder, then closed it again. Why even waste his time?

When the infant in Bradley's arms started to fuss and wiggle, Bradley smiled indulgently at his son. "Look who's awake in time to see Uncle Barron. Here, want to hold him?"

"No, I—"

"Sure you do. Nothing to it." Bradley slipped the blanket-wrapped infant into his arms. "Sam needs to get to know his new family."

Barron clutched the small bundle awkwardly.

*Please don't let me drop it.*

Before he could blink, the boy settled into the crook of his arm as naturally as if he had always been there. Dark eyes in a wrinkled red face flew open and fixed accusingly on Barron.

"Uh-oh," Barron said. "I think he knows I'm not you."

"It's good for him to get used to being held by different folk."

Barron remembered the story of how Bradley, as a newborn, had been left on the steps of a church with no one to hold him or welcome into the world. Small wonder he took the way he did to fatherhood.

"I wonder how my ma did it," Barron mused, as he stared down at the baby's wrinkled face and furrowed brow. When Sam scrunched his face, he looked more like a little old person than a newborn. "She had two of us at once to contend with."

"Mothers have special skills. I bet she managed just fine."

Just then Sam opened his mouth and let out such a howl Barron nearly dropped him. Not that he would, but how did so much noise come out of such a tiny mouth?

To his relief, Bradley scooped the baby back. "Looks like it's time to pass him back to his mama for a feed."

Barron watched Bradley make his way through the guests to his wife's side, aware his arms felt empty. Not unlike earlier, when Lily left him on the dance floor.

AT LONG LAST, the evening began to wind down. Standing at the kitchen sink as she washed dishes, Lily admired the way the yard looked all lit up with dozens of torches and candles. She saw why Rose chose to have her wedding here. For one thing, her sister would want nothing to do with a church wedding. And for another, the Copper Moon was Rose's new home, the first real home she'd had. What better way for Rose to start her new life with her new husband than invite friends and family to their home to celebrate?

The town ladies had politely included her in their conversation during the cleanup, but she was conscious of not being one of them. The Mason brides also were warm and welcoming as ever. But nothing could change the fact that she was an outsider.

Which was nothing new. She'd been an outsider all her life, along with Rose. Now Rose had her new family, and Lily was on her own.

Every time she heard Hawkes's name, a man she'd never met, she got the same sick, disgusted feeling as when she thought of their father. Each man was evil in his own way, except their father pretended to be doing good. It didn't sound as if Hawkes had any such delusions, which ironically made him the more honest of the two.

The window over the sink threw her reflection back at her. She knew what she wanted to do next. The question was, would she be able to pull it off? As she studied her troubled reflection, she realized that the yard, which had previously been festively alight, now lay in darkness and no one had come into the kitchen for a while.

She wiped her hands on a drying cloth and hurried outside. Surely Georgina hadn't left without her? But there was no sign of the café owner's buggy. In fact, there were no other buggies or carriages in the driveway. It seemed the entire population of Bullet had quietly crept away without her.

With the lanterns and candles extinguished, the yard no longer extended a friendly welcome. A slight breeze rustled the dry brush and added to the eerie isolation. Lily clasped her arms around her waist.

She wasn't totally alone, for she could see lights in the distance from the cabins occupied by the married couples. She turned back to the ranch house intending to grab a lantern and gasped when a shadowy figure stepped between her and the house, blocking her way.

Barron! She couldn't make out his features in the dark, but she instinctively knew it was him.

She raised her chin as she faced him. "You nearabout scared me out of my skin. Where is everyone?"

"The guests made a group pilgrimage back to town. From there, the newlyweds are continuing on to Yuma to have a night to themselves."

"Rose told me," she said.

"Did she also tell you she figured you ought to spend the night here at the ranch? She left your things upstairs in Brody's old room. Her and Bishop will be back tomorrow."

"I'm not staying here," Lily said. She didn't add "in the same house with you," but she certainly thought it.

"Rose didn't want you to be alone."

"Too bad!" Lily turned on her heel. Where she was going, she had no idea. Maybe over to Henrietta's cabin. Henrietta would understand. Henrietta would help her find a way back to town.

Barron caught her arm, effectively blocking her escape. "Rose hasn't let go of her 'big sister worry.' She said you had no place to go."

"Of course I do. I'm sure Georgina will let me stay in the empty room out back of the cafe."

"Did you ask her?"

Lily bit down hard on her lip. "Not exactly." She had simply assumed, something she wasn't about to admit to Barron. "I won't be sticking around for long, anyway."

Barron nodded. "Seems like a sound idea. Where will you go?"

*Good question. Where would she go?*

"Zara will have me back," she said, referring to the kind-hearted madam in Yuma who had taken pity on her once before.

"Is that the life you want?" he asked.

*Of course it wasn't.* She merely needed a way to buy herself some time and finalize her plan.

She shook off his hand. "If you'll excuse me, I'm going to ask Henrietta if I may borrow a horse to ride back to town."

Barron crossed his arms over his chest. "It's not safe out on the road alone in the dark. Why do you think everyone else headed out in a big group?"

Lily inhaled in frustration. "I don't imagine you would be so kind as to escort me back to town?"

Barron shook his head. "Not me. Two out there are every bit as vulnerable as one. Just ask Henny. Her and Percy were set upon, their horses stolen, Percy beat up and Henrietta taken as hostage."

"Henrietta was kidnapped?"

"Not exactly. As I recall she gave her captors the slip, then snuck around and stole her and Percy's horses back right out from under their noses."

"Of course she did," Lily said glumly. It sounded exactly like something Henrietta would do. Not lose her memory along with her ability to fight her way free the way Lily had.

She shot Barron a sideways glance. Was he doing it on purpose? Deliberately making her feel more inadequate than she already felt?

"I refuse to stay here alone with you. It's not seemly."

"It won't be just you and I here. Ben'll be back soon from seeing Georgina safe to the café."

"How come he can ride alone at night but you can't?" she said tauntingly.

"I didn't say I couldn't. I said I wasn't going to be responsible for you. That's the difference."

"Fine. I'll take my chances alone." She turned and flounced off toward the barn, aware of Barron following her.

"Just what do you think you're doing?"

"I'm going to borrow a horse. I'll return it tomorrow."

It was dark, but not too dark to see the way he pressed his lips into a thin line. "Brody will have my hide if I let you go out there alone."

She opened her mouth to say she didn't give a flying fig what Brody did, but he clapped his hand against her mouth before she could say a word.

"Sssshhhhh." He pulled her deep into the shadows near the entrance to the barn. She felt his breath, warm against her temple in the evening air, her spine against his chest. One strong arm, like a band across her middle, held her tight. The beat of their hearts, the rise and fall of their breathing sounded overloud in the quiet. In spite of herself, she felt her woman parts begin to soften. A tingle started low in her belly. Why did she have the sudden urge to turn toward him? To feel her bosom pillowed against his chest?

Then she saw what he saw. The jerky bob of lantern lights in the distance as several bodies moved through the underbrush on the north west side of the ranch.

Slowly he released her. "Can you shoot?"

She nodded wordlessly before she felt the cold steel of a revolver slide into her hand.

"Stay here. I'm going to circle around and try to come up behind them."

She saw him grab a rifle from the entrance to the barn before he melted into the darkness. She wanted to stop him. To tell him it was far too dangerous to go out there alone to face who knew how many intruders.

But she didn't say or do a thing. Only balanced the weight of the gun in her right hand and told herself she didn't care.

RIFLE IN HAND, Barron stayed low as he made his way soundlessly toward the source of the light. When it grew obvious that the lights were moving away from him, he hung back, not wanting to get too close. At one point, the intruders stopped and moved in a circle before heading in a different direction, toward the river.

"What brings anyone out here this late?" he asked under his breath. "Can't be anything good."

Seconds later, an arm was around his throat and a gun pressed to his temple.

# CHAPTER 3

Slowly Lily edged backward until her back collided with the side of the barn. She welcomed the solid feel of the wood behind her. Her knees were weak, and her heart was racing. The pistol in her hand felt like a lead weight.

She'd lied when she told Barron she knew how to shoot. Truth was, she'd never been in a position where she needed to aim a gun at anyone. And she didn't rightly know if she could pull the trigger. She hoped she could. She also hoped she never got put to the test.

In the distance the lanterns continued to flicker about; impossible to tell if they were growing closer or receding. All she knew was that someplace between her and the intruders, Barron was out there on his own. Defending her. Defending the ranch. Defending his family.

The knowledge sent tiny flutters through her. There was something so primal, so elemental about a man willing to risk all to defend what was his. She'd never come across it before, and the experience made her feel warm inside. Cherished. Like she mattered as a person, not just human chattel.

She had missed so much growing up. It was exciting to think she'd have a chance to not only learn about the ways of the world, and how others live, but to also do some good.

She was so deep in her thoughts she missed the sound of footfalls until they were right behind her. She froze when arms went around her, then instantly relaxed as she recognized Barron's touch, Barron's own unique scent. She might not trust him, but she instinctively knew he would never harm her.

"Did you find out who it was?"

"Not exactly," he said. "I ran into Brody and the others. They were the ones with the lights."

"What were they doing out there?"

"Same thing as me. They spotted movement and went to check it out."

She hadn't realized how tightly she still gripped the gun until Barron gently loosened her fingers and slid it from her grasp.

"What now?" she asked.

"We get you mounted up. Braydon and Blake will ride with us into town. Brody and Bradley will sit tight here at the ranch. Ben should be along anytime."

Lily bit her lower lip. It no longer seemed so imperative that she head back to town tonight. "I feel bad taking them from their wives."

Barron shrugged. "They're used to it."

"I don't mean to be a bother."

Barron gave a derisive snort. "Darlin', you've been a bother since we all first heard your name on Rose's lips. Why would that change all of a sudden?"

Stung, Lily followed him into the barn and grabbed a saddle. He'd called her "darling," but not like he'd meant it.

Not the way a man would address a woman he cared about. Not that it ought to matter one way or the other.

From Bullet, she could easily grab the stage coach into Yuma tomorrow. She had work to do.

Barron was up and about early the next morning, attacking the makeshift platform where the wedding and dancing had taken place. It felt good to grab hold of the hammer, dig in its claws to pry the boards apart, to hear the satisfying groan as nail released wood.

If only his thoughts of Lily could be so easily dismantled. Everywhere he looked, the ranch seemed full of memories of her sparring with him. Not to mention the way she'd felt in his arms while they danced. Later, having her angled against him in the dark out near the barn, his body had been keenly aware of every soft, shapely, fragrant inch of her.

"You're up early," Brody said as he strolled toward where he worked, a steaming cup of coffee in one hand.

"Someone has to be." Barron eyed the coffee longingly, figuring that must be one of the perks of having a woman in the house. He hadn't bothered to light the fire and make a pot for himself. As for Ben, there had been no sign of him when they escorted Lily into town. Maybe he'd stayed out all night. Barron hadn't bothered to check the other man's room. Figured Ben was grown up enough to not need watching.

Brody shrugged. "The baby's teething," he said. "She kept us up most of the night."

Barron blew out a breath as he felt his fists start to curl into balls. He longed to hit something powerful bad and could tell, from the way Brody watched him, that Brody knew exactly how he felt.

"Lots of things in this life can't be dealt with by a well-placed blow," Brody said mildly.

"And other things can."

"You manage to figure out the difference yet? Or are you saving that lesson for a different day?"

"What is it with everyone around here?" Barron felt as exasperated as he knew he sounded. "We all saw Hawkes kill Joe. We know he's wronged plenty of others. We swore an oath that night to take him down."

Brody nodded. "That's a fact. But there's a right way and a wrong way of doing things."

"There's also plenty of ways to kill a man."

Brody gave Barron a look he'd come to know well. The one he thought of as "Brody's look."

"Believe me, by the time we're done with that murdering, thieving lout he'll be better than dead. And every one of us will reap the satisfaction of watching him fall."

Barron went back to attacking the boards. "That's good. Started to worry you might have gotten soft. Too much baby stuff on your mind instead of the important stuff."

He saw Brody eyeing the way he ripped the nails from the boards.

"Take it easy on the wood, Barron. It can't hit you back. And we'll be needing to reuse it one of these days."

"Anticipating another wedding sometime soon?" Barron said cynically. "Is that why Ben never came home till late? If he came home at all."

"Hard to say what might happen." Brody changed the subject. "Laura noticed you never lit a fire this morning. She sent me to bring you up to the house for some breakfast."

Barron tensed. He'd never been invited into the cabins of

any of the newlyweds. Whenever everyone got together for a meeting or a meal it was down at the big ranch house. "Tell her thanks," he said curtly. "But tell her I got stuff to do."

"Suit yourself." Brody turned and headed back toward his cozy cabin where a plume of smoke curled lazily from the chimney and a hot meal waited. Barron heard his stomach rumble, aware that the empty feeling inside him had little to do with the fact that he hadn't yet eaten.

THE NEXT DAY, after Lily disembarked from the stage coach in Yuma, she made her way to Zara's. The town's madam didn't seem the least bit surprised when Lily walked into the kitchen without bothering to knock.

"Wondered how long before you'd be back." Zara swept one hand toward the coffee pot on the stove, a message Lily recognized from the time she stayed here before Rose and the twins found her.

Obediently she poured herself half a cup and topped up Zara's for her, then pulled out a chair. "Why do you say that?"

The older woman narrowed her gaze. "One gets to be a pretty good judge of character in my line of work. You didn't strike me as the type to sit around doing needle point out at the ranch."

"I haven't seen a single cross-stitch since I've been there," Lily said. "The wives all seem to have their own interests outside of their marriages."

"I'm glad to hear that. You come to say goodbye or what?"

"Not goodbye. Not yet," Lily said. She pressed her lips

together wondering how best to broach the subject that had been chasing around in her head, keeping her awake at night. "You know how the Masons have this ongoing feud with the man called Hawkes?"

Zara's face darkened. "That murdering cur killed a sweet little gal I knew and cared about, one who never hurt so much as a fly in her life. He got away with it, too. There's folks like him, just plain born evil. I'd love nothing more than to see him get what's due."

"And the twins want vengeance for him killing their brother."

"The twins aren't the only ones to suffer a loss at the hands of that no good S.O.B."

"Do you have any idea why he wants to take over Bullet and destroy the Masons? What's on their ranch that he's so desperate for?"

"Lots of theories about that. Plenty of drunken talk between Hawkes and my girls over the years, till I banned him."

"Go on," Lily said.

She felt the probe of Zara's kohl-rimmed eyes. "Why do you want to know so bad?"

"You know the twins helped Rose to hunt me down after I was kidnapped. She kind of made them a promise."

"Which is nothing to do with you." Zara blew on her coffee to cool it, but Lily could sense her interest.

Lily pressed her lips together. How to best explain the passion that burned inside her? "Our father was an evil man, all the more despicable because he pretended to be doing the Lord's work. Strikes me Hawkes is not so different, spreading terror and destroying the lives of innocent people."

"The sins of the father," Zara said. "You trying to somehow atone for your pa's misdeeds?"

"His actions make me sick. The same way I feel every time I hear Hawkes's name. Maybe one day I'll deal with my pa, but for now it strikes me I might be able to do some good before I leave town. If I succeed, it will not only make life better for my sister, but everyone else in these parts."

"A one-woman crusade?" Zara stared into space. "You need to know bad things happen to anyone who gets too close to Hawkes. Folks hereabouts know he killed his wife. Spent some time in jail but managed to eventually get off. Rumor is he headed up a gang of stage coach robbers back in the day, then killed them all to keep the spoils for himself. Because they suspected what he was up to, the others hid the loot before he got his hands on it. He killed them all without finding out where they stashed it."

"And maybe the stuff they stole is hidden someplace on the Copper Moon Ranch?" Lily said.

Zara shrugged. "No bodies were ever found. Poor Amanda's father rode with the gang. Heard tell the gal has a map her pa left her ma."

"A map to what?"

Zara shrugged. "The loot? The bodies? No one knows for sure, but Laura was nearabout killed trying to find out."

"You sure know a lot about the old days," Lily said. "I bet you have a secret or two of your own."

"Secrets not meant to be shared," the older woman said. "Be taking them to the grave with me."

Lily was filled with admiration for the woman before her who'd seen and done so much, yet hadn't let life harden her. "Will you help me?"

"Depends what you need."

As LILY DROVE her borrowed rig past the stage coach station in Yuma she heard a loud whistle, a familiar sound she would recognize anywhere. She glanced over at the station, where Rose stood alongside Bishop, who carried a small satchel.

Seeing the newlyweds, Lily felt herself blush clean to the roots of her hair. All the years she and her sister had shared a bed or a bedroll and now here was Rose, a married woman and newly initiated into mysteries of the marriage bed. She got hold of herself and pulled up with a jaunty wave. "Need a lift?"

The two of them hurried over. "We just missed the coach," Rose said. Rose's skin pinkened as she spoke, and Lily would have to be blind to miss the look in her sister's eyes as they rested lovingly on her new husband.

Lily couldn't imagine ever looking at a man that way. As if he'd hung the moon and the stars especially for her. "You're in luck. I'll take you in to Bullet." She glanced quickly over her shoulder to ensure the tarp still covered several carpetbags in the back which contained a variety of borrowed finery.

"Where did you get this rig?" Rose asked as Bishop helped her up and swung himself in after her.

"I borrowed it for a few days," Lily said vaguely.

Rose gave her a scrutinizing glance. "Borrowed it from who? You don't know anyone in Yuma."

Lily picked up the reins. "I've been making friends."

"That's great," Rose said. "I confess I was worried about you being here all on your own. Now that I'm ... Now that I'm not ...."

"Now that you're married and not going to be around all

the time like in the old days," Lily finished for her. Briefly she took one hand from the reins and patted Rose's hand where it sat in her lap. "You've been worrying about me forever. Now you've got Bishop to mother-hen over. Isn't that right, Bishop? You'll keep Rose so busy she won't have time to worry about me. I'm betting I hardly ever see her."

"I hope you'll always feel free to stop by the ranch whenever it suits you," Bishop said. "We can be a rowdy bunch, but there's always room for one more."

"Even though your brother hates me?"

Bishop cleared his throat. "Barron doesn't hate you."

"Despises me?" Lily asked.

"No one knows better than me that Barron can seem a bit difficult at times. He means well."

Lily sniffed. Told herself she didn't care one twiddle about Barron and his likes or dislikes. "He has a funny way of showing it. His good intentions, I mean."

Even as she spoke, she knew it wasn't true. She and Barron might be oil and water, but he had been almost kind last night when he'd seen her back to town. Of course, she knew the real reason he pretended to be nice was so he'd wind up seeing the back of her all the more quickly. Too bad for him she had plans to stick around a little longer.

When she drove to the Copper Moon to drop off her passengers, who was the first person she saw? None other than Barron. Bishop handed his bag to his brother and hopped out first.

"Eerie, isn't it?" Rose said, watching the two men. "Seeing them side by side."

Lily shrugged. She'd always thought as much. Wondered how Rose had known from the outset which twin had captured her heart.

"They're not so much alike, though," Rose added.

"Oh, I know that," Lily said jauntily. "You married the nice one. Unlikely Mr. Sour Cheeks will ever find a woman willing to put up with him."

~

BARRON COULDN'T RESIST. As Bishop helped his bride down and grabbed the overnight bag, he sauntered over to the driver's side of the rig.

"To what do we owe the pleasure of your company again so soon?" He was pleased to see a white line of displeasure pinch the corners of Lily's nostrils.

"Just being courteous and saving the newlyweds a nasty trip back in the stage coach. Not that you'd know anything about courtesy for courtesy's sake."

Barron patted the horse's neck without taking his eyes from Lily. "I take it this is fond farewells then?"

Lily shrugged. "Take it any way you want."

As if sensing the tension, Bishop wandered over to referee, the way he always did. He flung a brotherly arm across Barron's shoulder.

"Is that any way to talk to your new sister?"

Barron made a rude noise. "Your sister, bro. No sister of mine."

"Oh, come now," Lily said. "Bishop was just telling me how you're all one big happy family that I'm welcome to join in with any old time I feel like."

Barron turned on Bishop, fists clenched. "You told her *what?*"

"You heard Lily. I told her she's always welcome here on the ranch." His voice dropped an octave. "Welcomed by all of us."

Barron forced his fists to unclench. "What is this? Keep

your friends close and your enemies closer?"

Bishop grinned and clipped him playfully on the jaw. "Only one enemy in these parts. Soon to be no more, if things go according to plan."

"Plan?" Lily interrupted. "What plan?"

"Nothing that concerns you," Barron said tightly. But he narrowed his gaze. Something about the sudden level of interest he saw on Lily's face got his defenses marshaled. He'd known from the very start she was up to something. But what?

He blew out a breath, hardly able to wait till she drove away in her fancy new rig and never looked back.

As for the rig ... He gave it a second, closer look. How did Lily happen to be driving a buggy as new and modern as they came? The horse, as well, was a fine specimen.

His eyes narrowed. Where had Lily, who'd had nothing but the clothes on her back when they found her, got her hands on the means to be sporting such finery?

One thing was for sure. The lady was up to no good.

Lily shook with anger as she drove back to Bullet. Barron was the worst, most insufferable bully. She could just picture him years ago in the school yard, picking fights with the other kids, enjoying bloodying their noses and knocking them to the ground.

Not that she'd ever seen a schoolyard except in passing, mind. But still, she'd read enough over the years that she could paint a fairly accurate image.

Which led to her next dilemma. Where to stay. She wanted to remain here in Bullet for the time being, close to matters at hand.

Shame Henrietta wasn't further along in her plans to build a decent hotel. A project which, like many others, had been delayed because of Hawkes.

She pulled up in front of the café, climbed down and went inside, only to be greeted by the glum-faced cook Georgina had hired.

"Miss Georgina's not here," he said. "Her ma took a turn for the worse."

Georgina's mother, a long-standing member of the community hadn't been at the wedding yesterday, Lily recalled. Georgina had said she was at home resting. That she'd been feeling poorly of late.

Lily drove to Georgina's house on the next street over but when she turned the corner, she feared the worst. The undertaker's wagon was pulled up out front.

# CHAPTER 4

Hawkes returned home in a foul mood, just as the sun was rising. He blinked in the sudden brightness and ground the heel of one hand into the sand like grit of his eyes. That high-roller card player he only knew as "The Doc" had been in Yuma last night, and Hawkes had been feeling lucky. For a change, the cards had been going his way, and he'd been feeling mighty optimistic.

He still wasn't sure what happened. All he knew is that sometime after midnight his luck had changed, and there's been nothing he could do to get it back. As in the past, The Doc had graciously accepted his marker, but Hawkes wasn't stupid. As of this morning, he was into The Doc for far more than he was worth. Nothing for it but to figure his way into a sure-fire windfall of cash.

He'd lost all his partners in the mining venture, and they were already bleeding him dry with the interest payments on their original investment. The bank wouldn't give him the time of day and his lawyer was avoiding him as if he had the plague.

It was a far cry from the glory days when everyone came

around currying favor, bowing and scraping their way into his good books. He'd been on top before, and he'd see his way back there again through fair means or foul.

He smiled to himself. "Foul" being his favorite means.

Just outside of the barn he caught sight of Denim. Man had been nothing if not useless lately. Hawkes pulled up and remained mounted. Nothing made a man feel powerful like looking down on another. "You'd better have good news for a change."

"You'll like what I have to say," Denim said.

"Better than your useless report from the Mason ranch the night of the wedding?"

"I told you, there was nothing to report. By the time we got close enough to see what's what, the party was all packed up and long gone. I'm thinking the Masons must be getting soft if they can't stay up past dark. The guests had all scurried back into town as well. There was no fun to be had for me and the boys."

Hawkes resisted the urge to roll his eyes. As if Denim knew what fun was. "You had something to tell me?"

"Yup. Just heard tell there's a new gal in these parts. Quite the looker according to those who seen her. Rich, too. Word is her daddy just died and she's all on her lonesome."

"I got no time for some spoiled, rich snit," Hawkes sneered.

"You might for this one. She was asking around town who's the man in the know. Seems her daddy had some crazy last wish. Left her a bundle of cash in order to fulfill the dream in his memory."

"You even know what fulfill means?" Hawkes said.

"Sure," Denim said. "Means it'll be easy for you to tell her what she wants to hear."

"You find out where she's staying?"

"Not yet. Wanted to check with you first."

"Well find out. And make sure she doesn't get anywhere near those Masons." He leered. "Might be time I cleaned myself up and made a little call. Could turn out I knew her daddy in the old days."

"What old days?" Denim asked.

Hawkes spat on the ground, narrowly missing his foreman's dusty boots. "Will you ever learn when to shut up?"

"HAWKES WAS OUT ALL NIGHT," Barron reported to his twin.

"You kept watch all night?" Bishop said.

"May as well. Got no wife to keep me warm." But he grinned as he said it, letting Bishop know he was happy to see Bishop happy. "I might talk to some of the others about helping us keep watch."

Bishop gave his head a quick, decisive shake. "For now, the fewer who know we're watching Hawkes's place, the better. That'll all change once we have something concrete. Something we can make a plan with."

Barron nodded. "I sure would like to be a fly on the wall in that house."

"No luck getting any of the servants to spy for us?"

Barron shook his head. "They must be some scared of Hawkes. Every last one of them pretended not to speak English."

LILY PLACED a comforting arm around Georgina, feeling the woman's shoulders shake as she sobbed softly into her hankie. The brilliant overhead sunshine felt strangely at odds with the sad-faced, dark-garbed mourners clustered near the graveside in Bullet where the reverend spoke fondly of Georgina's parents, who had been among the earliest settlers to the area.

The preacher added how Georgina had been a mere babe in arms when the couple had started serving hot food from the back of their wagon to hungry newcomers. As the town grew, the couple had gone on to erect first a tent, then a shed, and eventually the popular café, which had been recently expanded and modernized by Georgina.

Lily found it strange the way Georgina had lived here her entire life, yet seemed so alone on today of all days. Georgina knew everyone, yet Lily had been the one she had turned to for comfort and support as the funeral arrangements were made, the burial site chosen, the plain wooden coffin delivered from Yuma.

Rose and her new sisters-in-law stood close by, forming a protective ring around Lily and Georgina. The Mason men had been pallbearers, bringing the coffin from the tiny overflowing chapel to the cemetery out back where mourners gathered who had not been able to cram inside the small church. Lily noticed the Mason men all wore the same black suits they had recently donned for Bishop and Rose's wedding.

"I should go check on things," Georgina whispered to Lily as the reverend finished up his eulogy.

"Not today," Lily whispered back. "Trust me when I say things are under control."

Ironic the way, times past, Georgina had been the one to feed the hungry hordes gathered for funerals, weddings, christenings and the like. Lily knew the townsfolk had been busy for days fixing food to serve those gathered to help console Georgina in her time of loss. By the time they moved from the cemetery to the town park, all was in readiness.

Lily still felt a bit funny about occupying the bedroom at Georgina's where her mother had recently passed, but when Georgina insisted she couldn't bear to be alone, Lily had reluctantly moved in, along with her borrowed props and finery. She had taken full advantage of the days leading up to the funeral in order to finesse her plan. And she was just about ready.

She wasn't used to accepting help from others, but in this instance, she knew she wouldn't have a workable plan without Zara's knowledge and assistance. From that good woman, she had also gleaned several interesting tidbits about the Masons themselves. By getting Hawkes out of everyone's hair, she would be doing the entire town a service.

"I see you're still here."

How had Barron managed to approach without her seeing him coming?

"Aren't you the observant one?" she said as she set down her teacup a little harder than necessary. Folks mingled about the park, chatting and picking at the eats, but no one was close enough to save her from Barron's company.

He stood staring down at her, arms crossed over his chest, eyes narrowed. If his tough-guy stance was his attempt to scare her away, he'd need to do a lot more than give her the evil eye.

"Way I was raised, funerals are for folks who knew the deceased more than a minute," he said.

"Funerals are also a day to comfort and support those

left behind," she said. "Not that you'd know anything about that."

His eyes narrowed further. "I know plenty about loss. And how it feels to be the one left. Powerless to save his—" He bit off his words abruptly and clamped his lips shut as if realizing he'd said too much. Shared something he had no intention of sharing. Least of all with her.

Lily slowly stood. Around her it felt as if the world had suddenly gone still. Background chatter of the other mourners faded to a mere wind blowing across the desert. "Do I detect a well-hidden sensitive side beneath all that bluster?"

He gave his head a shake and started to turn away. Shocking even herself, Lily reached out to stop him. She felt his forearm tense and saw the way his fists started to curl. The man really was accustomed to brawling his way out of any situation.

"Barron, what do you say to a truce? If not for us, then for them." She waved a hand to where the Masons had gathered near Georgina. "Believe me, I'll be on my way soon enough. In the meantime, it would be more pleasant to at least act civil any time our paths chance to cross."

"I'll do my best to prevent that from happening."

"What? Being civil?"

"Our paths crossing." Then he was gone, leaving her to stare at his retreating back. For a minute there, she'd sensed an almost human side to the man. Most confusing.

"Son of a—" Barron handed his spyglass over to Ben. He didn't need it's magnifying power to recognize the blonde guiding the fancy horse and carriage down the driveway toward Hawkes's palatial home.

Ben let out a low whistle. "What's she doing here, do you figure?"

"Rose's sister or not, I knew from day one she couldn't be trusted. Sweet little Lily may have managed to pull the wool over the eyes of the rest of them. I recognized her true colors right from the start."

He took the spyglass back and watched as Lily daintily climbed from the carriage and picked her way toward the front door. She was dressed in what Barron could only guess to be high fashion, unlike anything he'd seen on the women around Bullet.

Her matching tailored jacket and long skirt emphasized her hourglass silhouette. The suit was fashioned in a jewel tone of blue so bright it almost hurt his eyes, sides and seams trimmed with a stiff row of black ruffles. Bands of black lace ringed her delicate wrists. Atop her head perched the most outrageous bonnet he had ever laid eyes on, decorated with a wild collection of feathers and bows.

"She sure does clean up," Ben remarked.

"If you go for that overdone look," Barron said.

"Strikes me as a city look," Ben said.

"So," Barron mused more to himself. "What's a missionary's daughter from the back of beyond doing here at Hawkes's ranch, all tarted up like royalty?"

Ben clapped him on the shoulder. "You're right. She's up to something. And you, my friend, are the man who is going to find out what."

"How do you propose I go about that? The woman loathes me."

"You know what they say about love and hate."

"Strange bedfellows?" Barron said.

"The two are often more closely aligned than one might think."

LILY KNOCKED and took a deep breath as she waited for the door to be answered. If Hawkes wasn't in, she would have gone to a whole lot of bother for nothing.

She heard Zara's voice as plain as if the woman sat on her shoulder, guiding her. *Play to the man's ego. Flatter him. Let him think you're dazzled by his maturity and acumen. Let him know you're interested in a piece of what he's got going. But that you also have insider knowledge.*

The door was opened by a tired looking Mexican woman. "Jes?"

"Mr. Hawkes, please."

"I see." The door slammed leaving her standing on the porch.

Lily tapped her foot impatiently as the minutes marched past. She had just raised her hand to knock again when the door flew open and she stood face-to-face with the man she had heard so much about.

Gray stubble clung to his saggy jowls. His eyes were blood shot. His shirt buttons were done up wrong, as if he had just stuck his arms into the garment and buttoned it as he came to the door.

On catching sight of her, his scowl immediately shifted to a cunning, assessing grimace that she assumed was his attempt to smile.

"Well, well. And who might we have here?"

"Miss Lilith Mayberry. And do I have the pleasure of speaking to Mr. Guy Hawkes?"

He almost clicked his heels together and saluted. "At

your service, little lady." He swept his arm in wide half circle, a move Lily took as a feeble attempt at gallantry. "Pray step inside out of the punishing noonday sun before you spoil your beautiful complexion."

He ushered her inside, down a cavernous front hall and into a dark and over-furnished parlor. She chose the straight-back chair closest to the door, just in case. When he rang a bell, the same sad-faced Mexican woman scuttled into the room moments later.

"Might I offer you a refreshing beverage, Miss Mayberry? Perhaps some sweet tea to quench your thirst?"

Lily's stomach turned as she removed her gloves, finger by finger, aware of the predatorial way he watched her every move. He was even more despicable than she had expected.

"Sweet tea would be most welcome," she managed to say. Pretending to be dazzled by such a disgusting creature was going to be much harder than she had anticipated.

The woman nodded and left without a word, after which Hawkes made his way to a side table with several decanters and glasses and poured himself a generous portion of an amber liquid.

He turned to her and raised his glass. "You strike me as a lady who appreciates a mature man's tastes and appetites."

Lily shuddered at the inference, relieved when the housekeeper returned with her drink. She took a sip and set the over-sweetened tea on a nearby side table.

She raised her gaze to him. "Pray, sir. Do take a seat. For I'm also a lady who believes in getting straight to the point."

Hawkes let out an approving growl as he lowered his bulk to the settee. "A woman after my own heart. Never did cotton to this pussy-footing around. Straight from the hip. That's how I call 'em."

"Good. Then you'll appreciate what brings me here."

He leaned forward with a leer. "Whoever sent you my way, Miss Mayberry, I am eternally grateful."

"I expect you'll be even more grateful once you hear what I have to say."

She lowered her eyes for effect. "My dear Papa had a dream of coming west. Alas, he didn't manage to complete the journey. But he entrusted me to make his dream a reality."

Hawkes sat back. "I don't follow."

"'Invest in the west,' was his motto. His contacts had told him you were the man in the know in this particular area, and the locals certainly seem to agree."

"They do if they know what's good for them." He tried to make it a joke, but Lily had no doubt he meant every word. "What exactly held your dear daddy's interest?" Hawkes leaned forward, his eyes gleaming.

"Copper," Lily said. "Papa believed copper to be the gold of the future. He had it on good recommendation that there is a rich vein of copper in this immediate area. I understand you had several interested investors lined up. Investors who grew impatient and pulled their financial backing. Which tells me there is an opportunity here for a new partnership to be struck."

Hawkes gaze narrowed. "Afraid I don't partner with women."

"I heard that as well," Lily said. "I'm here to change your mind."

BARRON STARED at Hawkes's front door. What the heck could Lily be doing in there for so long?

"Come on, man, we have to get back," Benjamin said.

"Brody's expecting us."

Reluctantly Barron turned his mount and followed Benjamin back to the ranch. Lily was a big girl. More than capable of looking after herself. But he couldn't help remembering the time Bradley had taken off on his own to confront Hawkes and wound up as Hawkes's prisoner, locked in the root cellar and badly beaten before the rest of them found him.

He shrugged off the thought. Lily would be fine. He had no business worrying about her. None at all.

Brody looked up as Bishop and Benjamin entered the big ranch house. "Nice of you to join us." The others were already gathered around the big, scarred table that dominated the room. Barron felt his curiosity rise as he slid into the seat next to his twin. None of the women were in attendance, which meant this was a serious men-only meeting.

"I thought I'd take advantage of everyone being here right now to update you all on a few things going on." Brody cleared his throat and glanced around the table from man to man, as if making sure he had everyone's undivided attention. "We've been luckier than most folks in the area. While some of our neighbors have sold and moved on, and others struggled to make a living, we've prospered. We've created a demand for our beef out on the coast. Rail transport has increased our deliveries. But I sense the winds of change."

"Are we getting out of the cattle business?" Blake asked.

Blake had a brilliant mind for anything mechanical. As things became more automated, Barron had often wondered how much longer Blake would be hitting the trails with them. Likely there were many other things Blake could turn his talents to without leaving home.

"Not altogether," Brody said. "Not at this point. But the market is getting more competitive. I foresee a time in the future when cattle drives will become a thing of the past. Refrigeration on the rail cars means the beef can be butchered and shipped from almost anywhere in the territories."

There were a few murmurs of dissent from around the table as the men digested what Brody was saying. Barron got it. Change was never easy to accept, but he had always admired Brody's head for business. He knew Brody had diversified a lot of the ranch's profits by investing in the railways, among other things.

Braydon spoke up. "The town is growing. We plan to grow with it. Henrietta has started to build a hotel on the land where Amanda's family home was before the fire."

"Where does that leave us?" Bishop asked.

"What about Hawkes?" Barron piped up. Talk about the future was all very good and well, but he was more than ready to put paid to their nemesis once and for all.

Brody smiled. "Which brings me to our next topic. Hawkes is both greedy and stupid. I know a few of you—" his eyes found Barron—"from time to time have questioned the pace at which our plan is unfolding. And I want to let you know we're getting close. Hawkes's time is nearly up."

"What's that mean?" Barron asked.

"We," Brody said, "have been slowly, steadily, anonymously, buying up all of Hawkes's many mortgages and loans. He's drowning in debt, and when the time is right, we're going to cut off his air supply. We're just about ready to ruin the man. But we need to do more than financially destroy him. We need to publicly decimate and humiliate him, to rip out his guts and leave him broken and bleeding. Same way he's treated others."

"He's killed," Barron said. "Doubtless more folk than the ones we know about."

Brody nodded. "The reason I called everyone together is so that we can put our heads together and figure out a way to bring Hawkes to his knees in front of the entire town before we strike the final blow. In such a way as he doesn't see any of it coming. Any ideas?"

As he listened to the chatter around the table, Barron felt the dawning of an idea to end all ideas. But first he had to figure out if it was feasible. Perhaps little Miss Lily could be of some use after all.

# CHAPTER 5

Lily drove her borrowed rig from Hawkes's ranch to Bullet lost in thought, wondering if she might be in over her head.

*You can do this*, she reassured herself for the umpteenth time.

After all, hadn't she learned all about manipulative tactics from the best? Greed was greed, no matter what the currency. Her father's sickness had been born from a need for power and control. Hawkes's evil nature had a voracious appetite for money and power. She didn't know enough about the world to know why some men were that way, only that they needed to be stopped from preying on innocent victims.

When she had coolly pointed out to Hawkes how his clumsy tactics to gain title of the Copper Moon had gotten him exactly nowhere, he'd vehemently denied it. But facts were facts. He'd struck out every time he tried to get his hands on the ranch, dating back to the days of the old uncle before Brody arrived on the scene.

She couldn't have done any of this without Zara's help.

Lily knew she had her work cut out to convince Hawkes she could deliver the ownership deed after all the times he'd failed. Still, he had all but drooled at the prospect of her infiltrating the family by making friends with the brides and seducing one of the brothers. Seduction was likely the only thing Hawkes considered women good for.

By the time she had finished delivering her proposal, he had actually stood to shake her hand, which she immediately longed to wash. Just being in the same room with the man made her feel repulsed and soiled, and she was imagining soaking in a nice, hot bath when she heard the heavy pounding of hooves coming up behind her.

She glanced over her shoulder. Barron! Where was he off to in such a hurry?

She slowed and pulled to the side of the road, giving him plenty of room to pass. Instead, he slowed up and drew abreast of her. His sideways glance met hers with a forceful wallop, almost as if he knew what she'd been up to. She pulled on the reins and brought the rig to a halt.

He pushed back the brim of his Stetson with one knuckle as his horse pranced alongside her carriage, giving him the advantage of looking down on her.

"Did you mean what you said the other day about a truce?"

She nodded.

"In that case, what were you doing at Hawkes's place just now? The two of you all chummy."

Lily eyed him carefully, but he gave away nothing. Had he been watching her? Or Hawkes?

"As you know, Hawkes is not someone to get chummy with. We were discussing a business opportunity."

"If you're thinking about throwing your lot in with his,

you're making one H of a mistake. He's going down, and you'll go with him."

She pressed her lips together thoughtfully. Barron didn't know it yet, but she needed him. "Why would you care? Strikes me as you'd be happy to watch me go up in flames."

"You're Rose's sister. I thought I'd try appealing to your better nature. If you have one."

The man was by turns insufferable, exasperating and frustrating. But he could also prove useful. She patted the seat next to her. "Why don't you join me on the driven into town? I'll tell you my secrets if you tell me yours."

She smiled inwardly as confusion played across his features. Clearly, she had caught him off guard.

After a brief hesitation, he dismounted, tied his horse to the back of the rig and swung himself up next to her with a squeak of carriage springs. His leg brushed hers in a slow, deliberate move, as if to emphasize he was bigger and stronger.

Lily flicked the reins and the buggy started forward. "You don't strike me as a man who's comfortable with a woman in the driver's seat."

He sat back, trailing his arm across her seat back. He was purposely crowding her, goading her. She couldn't let it get to her.

"One thing I've learned over the years," he drawled, "is never take a woman at face value. There's always more going on below the surface than what a lady lets on."

At least he'd called her a lady. "Is that so?"

"That's been my experience."

"Is that why you don't trust women?"

"I trust some women. When it's warranted."

"But not me."

"You least of any woman in my acquaintance."

"May I remind you, you sought *me* out today," she said sweetly. "I was simply going about my business."

"No, you weren't. You were in a powwow with Hawkes. Which makes it Mason business."

She took her time responding. She only had one chance to sell this. "Are you aware there's a rich vein of copper on the Copper Moon ranch?"

He did such an abrupt about-face he nearly fell from the carriage. Clearly he had no idea. His gaze narrowed.

"Who told you that?"

"Zara. Apparently old Dan Mason shared more than a few things across the pillow in his younger days. Hawkes confirmed it just now. Claims to have the assayer's report."

"Brody would know if that was the case. We all would."

He fell silent, and she left him to digest what she had said. She could almost hear the wheels turning in his brain as he examined this new information from all sides.

"Why would Brody keep something like that from us?" he finally asked.

"I'm sure he has his reasons. The way Zara explained it, old Dan was afraid of what would happen to the town if word got out. Fortune seekers would descend on the entire area. Shantytowns would spring up overnight, attracting unsavory elements. Law and order would disappear. And once the mine was tapped out, there'd be nothing left of his peaceful town but a mess."

"Hmmmm," Barron said.

Lily didn't point out the obvious. How Hawkes had been obsessively fixated on the ranch in a way that spoke to something far beyond a simple land grab or a cache of stolen loot.

"I hope you're not planning on spreading this around," he said finally.

Lily shook her head. "Nothing in it for me."

"How is it Hawkes knows all this?"

"That I don't know. I do know he had several partners lined up who got tired of the delays and empty promises. They eventually pulled out when he didn't deliver the title to the ranch and begin mining."

Barron nodded more to himself. "And he had to pay them back."

"Exactly," Lily said. "He's tapped out. Wouldn't be able to do a thing right now even if he did somehow get his hands on the ranch."

"Oh, yes he could," Barron said. "He could sell the mineral rights to the highest bidder and cause havoc in the area, which is his specialty. Overnight we'd see prices of everything double and triple. He'd force the locals out of business and out of town. Hawkes would essentially own and control Bullet and everyone here."

"Sounds like that's been his plan all along," Lily said.

Barron shifted in order to look her straight in the eye. She was conscious of his arm slung across the back of the seat between them, the warmth from his hand finding its way toward her. Suddenly she felt heated up from the inside out.

"If he's looking for a new partner, you're not much of a bet. Unless you robbed a bank since you've been here."

"Hardly my style," she said.

"Speaking of style, what's this all about? Fancy rig. Town clothes. Putting on fancy airs."

She smiled. "Don't tell me you've forgotten Rose's original proposal when she enlisted your help to find me? That once I was located, I could play the role of a wealthy heiress to gain Hawkes's trust?"

"Bishop and I killed the whole idea as soon as she suggested it."

"Maybe at some point Rose happened to mention it to me. And I found merit in the plan."

"Oh no!" Barron shook his head vehemently.

"Oh no, what?" She raised a brow.

"You're going about this all wrong. Bishop and I were going to take on the bulk of the scam. No way would we let you be anywhere near the line of fire."

*Let her! As if she needed permission!*

"Well, I've gone ahead and laid the foundation. Hawkes was fairly salivating at the prospect of my proposal when I left him earlier."

"You don't know who you're dealing with. He's dangerous."

"Well then." Lily batted her eyelashes and leaned close. "I guess it'll be up to you to keep me safe."

FOR ONCE, Barron's hands didn't ball into fists as he faced the frustrating woman next to him. Instead he pulled her the last few inches into his arms and kissed her. Even as he lowered his mouth to hers, he had the distinct feeling that he had somehow played right into her hands. That she wanted him to kiss her.

The kiss had been a long time coming. Starting with the first time he laid eyes on her. What had Ben said about love and hate being closely linked? Was that why he'd gone out of his way to find fault and antagonize her? To squelch the way he truly felt?

As her mouth moved tentatively beneath his like she

wasn't sure what was expected, he realized this was likely her first kiss. And it was up to him to make it memorable.

When he whisked his tongue against the seam of her lips, she opened to him as naturally as if she'd been doing it her entire life. When her tongue shyly darted out to duel with his, he was lost. Drowning in her scent and her essence.

His hands smoothed the fine silk of her jacket, tracing the delicate curve of her spine as her breasts pillowed his chest. He was barely aware they had stopped moving, totally immersed in the fit and feel of her in his arms and the way her heat enveloped him, sending need churning through his blood stream.

He was mentally planning his next move when she gently ended the embrace. When she pulled back and eyed him in a calculating way, Barron felt as if he was being graded on a school exam, one that included his recent performance.

"That's good," she said, more to herself as she nodded. "Very convincing to anyone watching. I was worried you might not be able to fake actually liking me enough to fool the others."

"What are you talking about?" He felt fuzzy-headed, as if all the blood in his body had drained to one particular spot, leaving his brain starved of oxygen. "What others?"

She picked up the reins and resumed their trip. "Hawkes for one. He has to believe you've fallen hard for me."

"Why?"

"It was either you or Benjamin, as you're the only two bachelors left. I figured you and I had enough fire between us to make such a ruse work. I bragged to Hawkes that once I had you I'd be able to get you to do anything, including have Brody put the ranch in your name which you, in turn, would sign over to Hawkes when I tell you to."

"Why would he believe such a thing?"

"Simple. Because he wants to. He's egotistical enough to believe it can be that easy."

"You think you're smart, don't you?" Barron said.

Her lips curved in a bitter half smile. "I've dealt with his type before."

"Do you have any idea what Hawkes has done to this family? How his insidious evil has permeated everything and everyone we care about?"

"I understand you hate him more than I do, with good cause. All the more reason we do this together. Rid the world of the worst kind of evil." She patted his knee. "I knew we could agree on something if we put our minds to it."

"I suppose you planned all this?"

"What? You coming along and kissing me today? How could I possibly plan that?"

He had no answer. He'd only seen her earlier because he'd been watching Hawkes's place, and not until the family meeting today with Brody and the others did he decide to seek her out. Despite the conflicting feelings churning around inside him, he still didn't trust her farther than he could throw her.

"Truth is, we're almost ready to take Hawkes down. I planned to ask you to help us. If you were still around."

"Was kissing me part of your plan? You know, having me fall under your spell so I'd do whatever you wanted."

"Yeah," he said shortly. "It's working out real good so far, you being all meek and acquiescent and all."

"My, what big words, Mr. Mason. I bet those impress the girls as much as your kisses."

How had the conversation veered so far out of his

control? Kind of like her driving the buggy and him running behind. He was smart not to trust her. If only he didn't feel like pulling her back into his arms for another kiss.

"Things won't happen overnight," he warned her. "Our plans are just getting started."

He jumped when Lily patted his hand where it rested on his knee. "Don't you worry about me. I'll be just fine. Helping take down Hawkes and his kind is something I was meant to do."

"WHAT ARE WE DOING OUT HERE?" Bishop asked.

Barron blew out a breath. "Checking out some stuff."

Marriage had changed his twin. In the old days, Bishop would have followed along, unquestioning, with whatever he suggested. Like today's ride, far from the ranch and from the others.

Bishop pulled up. "Do you mind being a little more specific? You haul me out here without any explanation and expect me to blindly follow. The old days are over. I have a wife. Responsibilities. Heading off on some undisclosed secret mission is—" His words were cut off by a bullet whizzing between them.

Barron grabbed his weapon, dismounted, and dove for cover behind a boulder, reassured Bishop had reacted the same.

When there were no more shots, Bishop sent him a long, searching look that Barron didn't quite meet.

"Any chance you happen to know who's out there and why they're not exactly welcoming us with open arms?"

"I have a couple theories 'bout that," Barron said.

"I'm dying to hear," Bishop said. "Okay, not dying," he amended. "But all ears."

"I happened to hear a rumor recently that there could be copper somewhere on the ranch."

Bishop faced him unblinking, clearly not impressed by his news. "You run it by Brody?"

"Nope. Because I recalled something from back when Percy and Henrietta were on their hunt for the sunken ship of pearls. I overheard Braydon say to Brody that Henrietta was pretty sure she saw recent markings in the caves up above the cliffs."

"What kind of markings?"

"Marks that looked like they were made by an assayer. Brody brushed it off right quick and I didn't think any more of it till recent. But if Brody and or his uncle knew there was copper, stands to reason others folks could know as well."

"Which doesn't explain who's out there shooting."

Barron shrugged. "Obviously someone who doesn't want us near the place."

"Hawkes?"

"More like someone on his payroll, I'm thinking."

"Wait!" Bishop said, as if the thought just struck him. "You figure the presence of copper might be the reason Hawkes is so hell bent on owning the ranch?"

"It's the one thing that makes sense, given the way he's been trying to drive us off the land since forever."

"Much as I'd love to check out your theory, today doesn't strike me as we have much chance of getting any sort of closeup look."

Barron gave a longing glance over to where the shots had originated. "We could circle around behind the shooter."

"There's bound to be more than one." Bishop straightened and snapped his fingers for his horse. "Do you even know for sure we're in the right place?"

Barron shrugged. "The fact that someone's standing guard points that way."

"I've got a wife to get back to. You and I both have a family that kind of appreciates it when we get home in one piece."

Barron fell silent. Would he ever feel as close to the other brothers as Bishop did? Bishop's roots were dug in here deep, yet Barron felt like once Hawkes was out of the way for good, he could just as happily move on. Even though moving on without Bishop would be strange.

BRODY WATCHED Barron and Bishop cautiously looking around as they mounted up and rode back the way they came. Just his luck the twins would show up the same day he was out here trying to cover up the telltale marks in the cave. Truth be told, he didn't know how much longer he could keep his deathbed promise to Uncle Dan. Someone had ordered the testing done to determine the presence of copper in the area. No doubt others were privy to the results.

"ROSE IS mighty happy Lily's still in town," Bishop said, once they were out of firing range and on their way back to the ranch house. "I was hoping that didn't prove a problem for you."

Barron shrugged. "Safe to say Lily and I worked ourselves out an agreement of sorts."

"What kind of agreement?"

Barron met Bishop's look square on. Not much got by his twin. Bishop knew he wasn't much for amicable agreements, preferring to settle things with his fists. He blew out a breath, wondering just how much to confide.

"You can't tell Rose any of this. Swear on Joe's grave."

Bishop swiped his forearm across his forehead. "That serious?"

"Remember when Rose needed our help to find Lily? Came up with some cock-and-bull idea to have Lily charm Hawkes, pretend she had means?"

"Dumb idea," Bishop said. "We both agreed on that right out."

"Yeah, well, someone neglected to tell Lily it was a dumb idea. She took hold and ran to Hawkes with it."

"You need to stop her! Lily has no clue what Hawkes is capable of."

"It's too late for that. She baited the trap, and he took it."

"What do you mean?"

"For a missionary's daughter, Lily must be some mighty convincing liar. Hawkes believes she's someone whose rich pa just died, and her pa's dream was to invest in copper. She told him she wants to partner with him and honor her pa's last wish."

"Don't tell me!"

"Crazy as it sounds, there's a good chance it can work. Lily wants her and me to act all smitten in love. I'm supposed to be so crazy about her I'll do anything, including trick Brody into signing the ranch over to me. Which in turn I passively hand over to Lily, who's supposedly in cahoots with Hawkes."

Bishop gave his head a brief, dismissive shake. "It'll never fly."

"It doesn't need to fly. All that has to happen is to take things far enough where everyone in town is gathered together as Brody and the rest of us denounce and discredit Hawkes. Maybe even have that marshal standing by. Sadly, Hawkes gets himself killed in the aftermath."

"How do you plan to get the entire town together? Fake a wedding?" Bishop said.

Barron started to smile. "A wedding! That could work."

"I wasn't serious. Who the heck could pull it off enough to fake getting married?"

Barron shrugged. "Two brothers falling for two sisters? Folks'd buy that. If not a wedding, how about a party announcing their happy betrothal?"

"How do you plan to pull something off like that when you and Lily can barely stand the sight of each other?"

"I heard something just the other day about love and hate being kissing cousins."

Bishop snorted. "Sounds like a load of hogwash to me." His expression softened. "Since it doesn't sound like I'm able to change your mind, what can I do to help?"

Barron smiled. Good to have his brother back. "Just have my back, the way you always do. The others might be a little more difficult to convince. You can help with that."

LILY WORRIED SHE'D made a mistake listening to Barron. After all, what guarantee did she have that he would honor his word to have her involved? She hadn't seen hide nor hair of anyone from the Copper Moon in nearly a week. Could this whole charade have been Barron's plan to keep her out of the way?

Zara had warned her Hawkes had spies everywhere,

which meant she had to keep a low profile around Bullet. Be someone she wasn't. She certainly couldn't be seen as chummy with Georgina so had moved into Zara's fancy house on the outskirts of Bullet. The two or three nights a week when Zara's girls came from Yuma to work, she stayed in her room and tried to block out the noise of what went on all night. Unfortunately, the unmistakable sounds of physical encounters between a man and a woman reminded her of Barron and the kiss they had shared.

She'd heard a woman never forgot her first kiss, and she certainly wouldn't be forgetting that one. She'd felt him shudder, as if he was hanging on to control by a thread, so she must have done something right. Or maybe men were always that close to the edge. She heaved a sigh. So much she still had to learn.

As the days passed, she became convinced that Barron had deliberately blown her off, which threatened her plan to string Hawkes along. Fed up with waiting on Barron, she made her way to the Women's Institute in search of Henrietta. Henrietta, who was everything she wasn't. Well-to-do. Well-traveled. Independent and adventuresome.

She believed if any of the brides knew what was going on with Project Hawkes, as she thought of it, it would be Henrietta. Upstairs in the hall, she stuck her head into the room that served as an office and pulled it back out immediately. Slowly she backed down the hallway. They were all in there. The Mason brides. Their babies. A world so foreign to Lily, it could have been the moon.

Before she reached the stairway, she bumped into Rose. "Lily, there you are! I was looking for you. You weren't at Georgina's, and she said she hadn't seen you all week."

Lily forced a smile. "Here I am. You found me." Her sister had never looked so happy. Her eyes shone and her face glowed, with her smile stretched wider than Lily had ever seen.

Rose tilted her head. "What's with the fancy clothes?"

"It's a long story," Lily said.

"Come on." Rose took her arm and guided her back toward the office. "The other women were just asking what you were doing and I was embarrassed to say I didn't know." She stroked Lily's arm. "I've been so wrapped up with Bishop and settling into married life, I fear I've neglected you."

Lily shrugged. "I managed to keep busy."

"Storm is getting ready to take the book-lending wagon out with Blake and she's leaving me in charge of the library here," Rose said proudly. "Maybe you can help me. It would give us a chance to spend some time together."

Lily thought quickly. It seemed unlikely Hawkes would frequent the library. And he did expect her to get friendly with the Masons as part of the proposed scheme.

"Possibly," she said.

"I found her," Rose announced as they joined the others, where Lily found herself enveloped in multiple hugs, overwhelmed by the genuine caring in the way she was greeted. Almost as if she was one of them. Her eyes misted over as she glanced from one to the other. She *was* doing the right thing. Even if it meant pretending to be enamored with Barron.

"I'm so glad you're here," Henrietta said. "We're trying to make plans without the men around."

Lily blanched. "Plans for what?" Was it possible they knew what she and Barron had been talking about?

Henrietta's smile was wide and enthusiastic. "First there's the hotel, which I hope will be finished in time for New Year's."

"Henrietta wants to host a grand opening with a huge dance on New Year's Eve. One with the entire town in attendance," Rose said.

Lily glanced at Rose. Growing up, neither of them had studied a calendar to know what month it was, let alone plan a celebration on a certain occasion. All Hallow's Eve had been a totally overwhelming experience, one that was still fresh in her mind.

Laura spoke up. "Before Christmas and New Year's, we need to plan Thanksgiving."

"Thanksgiving?" Lily asked. She vaguely recalled some of the native tribes would plan a special harvest celebration in the fall, but it wasn't something she or Rose had experienced firsthand. Their father thought anything involving the native people smacked of heathenism.

"I've already told Brody no one is to be away on a cattle drive. As a family, we have much to be grateful for, and we need to be together to help celebrate."

Rose squeezed Lily's hand. "I'm so glad you're here to be part of all this."

Lily nodded and listened with half an ear as the ladies chatted about the upcoming feast they planned to prepare. She'd never seen a turkey, let alone tasted one.

All she knew was she and Barron had to put things in place with Hawkes before the festivities. Otherwise she was afraid Hawkes would wreak havoc and the celebrations would be disrupted. Or worse.

# CHAPTER 6

"The new gal's over in the hall with them others. You know, the fancy one from the city. That strike you as odd?"

Hawkes's gaze slid sideways to Denim. The man was getting to be a menace. "Everything that involves the Masons is worth keeping watch on."

"Something funny about that gal. Reminds me a bit of the one got Haywire killed."

Hawkes let out a snort. "You been smoking peyote with the Injuns? Gal Haywire tangled with was a runaway. You told me yourself the city gal in there is the real deal. Her rich pa died and she's looking to spend his money."

Denim picked his teeth. "You got a plan to help her with that?"

"Her and me got ourselves a sweet little business arrangement. Could turn into more, if you take my meaning."

Denim shrugged. "Whatever you say, boss. Long as you know what's going on around here."

Hawkes smiled to himself. Ever since he'd been deliberately staying away from the Masons, he was enjoying watching them become over confident.

"The bigger they are, the harder they fall," Hawkes said. "Let's go find us a card game. I'm feeling a visit from lady luck."

~

BARRON STRODE into the library room at the Women's Hall in Bullet. After one brief scan of the room, he spotted Lily shelving books in the back. Giving an acknowledging nod to Rose as she looked up from the book she was reading to a small group of children near the front, he made his way to Lily's side.

Lily gave him a haughty look. "Looking for some reading material, Barron?"

He took hold of her arm a little rougher than he intended and pulled her around the corner, out of earshot of her sister. She stared coldly at his fingers clasped around her upper arm until he released her.

"Sorry." He took off his hat and ran a hand through his hair. The woman made him crazy. "I've been hunting you down for days now."

"I've been busy."

"I don't even know where you're staying."

"Why would you need to know that?"

"I don't like you spending so much time with Hawkes."

She kept her face impassive, even as her eyes shot daggers into his. "It's not up to you who I spend time with. Hawkes is disgusting, but being around him, playing to his ego, is the only way I know to convince him I'm in this with him. Besides, the man has his uses."

Barron felt his fists start to curl. "What sort of uses?"

"I convinced him to show me the report from the assayer. He can barely read most of it, much as he pretends otherwise."

"And?" Barron prompted.

"And according to the report, the ranch is home to a very rich vein of copper."

Barron's breath whistled between his teeth. "Do you know where?"

"The report didn't say. I'm working on getting him to take me there."

"I want to be there, too."

"It's too soon. I'm still gaining his trust. If I show up with one of the Masons, everything goes for naught."

"How do you plan to convince him you can turn over the deed to the ranch?"

"He believes he and I are a team. Out to best the Masons, because they're in the way of what my daddy would have wanted."

"So you're not playing fair with me?"

"Not so far as Hawkes knows. Acting like I'm not repulsed by the man is no easy feat. The way he treats his staff is disgusting. It reminds me of my father's attitude toward the native tribes he was claiming to save from an eternity of hell and damnation."

"You shouldn't be out in the wilds, alone with him. He's already tried to harm several of our women." He clamped his lips shut, wishing he could take back his words, but it was too late. His words weren't lost on Lily, as attested by her provocative smile.

"Am I one of your women, Barron? Is that what I just heard?"

"I didn't mean it that way," he muttered, aware of just

how close they stood together. He tried to take a step back only to find himself locked tight against the bookshelf.

Meanwhile, Lily was in front of him, kissing close. Smelling as pretty as she looked. Her blue gown emphasized the cornflower blue of her eyes. Her blond hair was partly pulled back and secured with a ribbon. Softly curling strands clung to her bosom and emphasized her feminine curves.

His mouth felt dry, his breathing erratic.

"Funny," she said. "It sounds like maybe you're starting to care about me."

Was it his imagination or did she edge even closer? Tempting him? Provoking him? Daring him?

Her lips were impossibly close. Kissing soft.

He blinked and the moment was gone. If it had even been there to start with, and not just in his imagination. Lily stepped back, grabbed a couple more books off the cart and turned back to her task.

This madness had to stop. He'd come powerful close to kissing her. Here in the library. In front of her sister and anyone else who happened along.

"I'm done here for the time being." She turned to him as if nothing had happened. "Do you want to walk over with me and take a look at how the hotel's coming along?"

Shoot, he'd clean forgotten all about the hotel, even though it was all he heard about when the family got together lately. That and Thanksgiving, which would soon be followed by Christmas. Life at the ranch had seemed an awful lot simpler when it had been bachelor digs all the way.

Still, showing interest in the hotel would see him in the good graces of Henrietta as well as Braydon, even if it meant being in Lily's company at the same time. He'd been as fretful as one of the babies cutting a tooth when he was unable to locate her.

Now she was within spitting distance and all he could think about was hightailing it in the opposite direction. He gave his head a shake and put his hat back on. What on earth had come over him lately? Seemed like everything familiar had been turned on its keister.

Except the need to see Hawkes taken down and dead. That was the one constant in his life.

"Sure thing," he said. "High time I poked my nose over that direction."

Lily gave a light, teasing flick of her fingers to his nose. "Then bring that handsome nose of yours and let's go."

Barron did a double take. Did she just call him handsome? Was she playing him?

"We're heading to the hotel," she called to Rose. "We won't be long."

Rose, still engrossed in reading to her young charges, gave a distracted wave.

Once outside, Barron felt like he'd been sleeping for a long while and had just woken up. The town appeared busier than usual. Or maybe he just hadn't been in town for a while. People darted across the street from shop to shop, while women lugged baskets of goods to either buy or sell. Wagons from neighboring ranches lumbered past and discharged their passengers. Several of the buildings appeared to be sporting a fresh coat of paint.

As they reached the corner, the sound of banging hammers grew louder, punctuated by shouts from the workers. When they turned the corner, he stopped in his tracks.

Last time he'd seen Amanda's family home, he'd been on a bucket bigrade with most of the town in a futile attempt to douse the flames caused by an explosion and stop them from spreading to the property next door. Today, occupying the site of both ruined homes, the skeletal outline of the new hotel rose three stories high.

"Not wasting much time, are they?"

"Henrietta is determined to see the hotel open in time for the holidays. She offered the crew a bonus if they can meet her deadline."

"Money's a motivator," Barron said. "Is it me, or does the entire town have a more prosperous air to it than it used to?"

"I'm a relative newcomer, but I think what you're seeing is more like optimism," Lily said. "Hawkes hasn't been around threatening or strong-arming folks. No one's heard a peep from him in quite some time. There's been no tripping over dead bodies."

"Or he's gotten better at covering his tracks," Barron said.

To his surprise, Lily tucked her arm through his in a move that seemed purely natural and unaffected, as if she wanted to be arm in arm. He dropped the thought immediately. More like it was an act for Hawkes and his spies.

"Trust you to think like that," she said. "Let's go see how things are coming along inside."

"You sure you can trust her, boss? I mean, she's looking pretty darn friendly with the Masons these days."

Hawkes shook his head in Denim's direction. The man was getting more unpredictable all the time. It was past time to start grooming his replacement.

"Her and me got this all worked out. She's my means to getting my hands on the ranch."

Denim shook his shaggy head. "You also said she was bringing you luck with the cards."

Hawkes let out a growl of displeasure. Like he needed to be reminded of his latest losses. He'd been doing his best to tap Miss Lilibeth for some good-faith money, but so far she'd kept her purse strings shut tighter than a nun's chastity belt.

All of a sudden it struck him. He knew exactly what he needed to do in a show of good faith. One she couldn't help but reciprocate.

"You wait here," he told Denim. "First chance you see her alone, you tell her I need to see her at the house. To share some important developments."

"Then what?" Denim asked.

"You high tail it back before her. I'll be waiting to tell you exactly what to do next."

LILY HOPED that if she was spotted with Barron, it would spur Hawkes to move things forward. She didn't know how much longer she could stall his greedy moves to get his hands on the money she had led him to believe was readily available and at her disposal.

Barron's glower in no way resembled the look of a man who was well and truly smitten, delighted to be in the company of his intended. Before they went inside the framed structure, she tugged on his arm until he had no choice but turn and face her.

She smiled up at him. "Pretend you're enjoying my company," she said from the corner of her mouth. "You never know who might be watching."

With seeming reluctance, he took her in his arms. She

could feel the gallop of his heart as she pressed her fingertips to his chest. He was flushed and breathing heavy. Could it be due to her?

Gently she reached up and tugged at the corners of his lips, coaxing them into some semblance of a smile. Unable to resist, she stroked his lower lip with one fingertip. As if sensing a challenge, he parted his lips and dampened them with the tip of his tongue. She shivered at the sensation and teasingly dipped one fingertip inside his mouth, seeking his damp heat.

Having her finger in his mouth did funny things to her from the inside out. Her breasts started to tingle. An unfamiliar ache started low in her belly and spread to her limbs. His eyes were watching her, heavy-lidded with desire as she removed her finger. Instead, she curled her fingers through his hair and stood on tiptoe to press her lips to his.

"So that's the way of things, is it?"

Barron pushed her away at the sound of Braydon's voice. Disappointment churned through her. She'd been looking forward to his kiss. To learning a little more about the reaction he stirred up when he looked at her that way.

Henrietta stood next to Braydon, a wide grin across her face. "I think, my dear, we may have interrupted something."

Barron cleared his throat before he slanted Lily an unfathomable look. "Lily was keen to get over here and check things out. Thought I'd tag along."

Henrietta's grin widened. "Sure you did. Braydon always used to kiss me when he was tagging along on our dig site."

Lily didn't miss the way Braydon winked at Barron when he thought no one was looking. She hurried to Henrietta's side. "Are things on schedule to be ready for the holidays?"

Henrietta crossed her middle finger over her index finger. "Barring any delays, yes."

Lily had seen the sketches, but it was very different to walk through the roughly framed rooms, to imagine the finished product as Henrietta described architectural and decorative details. Trailing behind, Braydon and Barron appeared deep in conversation.

"I can't wait to see it all finished," Lily said to Henrietta. "I've never seen anything being built from the ground up, let alone on this scale."

"It's not for the faint of heart," Henrietta said. "But Braydon has been my main supporter. With him by my side, I truly believe I can accomplish anything."

"Didn't you feel that way before you married Braydon?"

"Not so much," Henrietta said. "As a woman, I was constantly being challenged at every turn. As a woman with the sanction of the man in her life, let's just say things have a way of going easier."

Lily's jaw dropped. "That's not right."

"Don't misunderstand me," Henrietta said. "I could have done this on my own just fine. Having Braydon's help doesn't weaken what I'm capable of accomplishing. On the contrary, having him by my side strengthens everything I do. And the same for him. Marriage truly is a partnership."

Lily fell silent, thinking on the unlikely partnership she had struck with Barron. Different as they were, they were united in their desire to best Hawkes. And Henrietta was right. It felt better to not take on the world all on her own.

"Do you and Braydon ever find there are some things that are impossible to accomplish? Even for the two of you?"

Henrietta's face said it all. "One of my toughest lessons ever. Learning to accept there will be some things I simply cannot change, no matter how hard I try. Not even with the joint effort of Braydon and myself together."

Lily didn't think that sounded like a fun lesson at all.

Outside the hotel, Lily and Barron parted ways. As if by mutual agreement, there was no touching or close proximity. Barron hurried off as if the hounds of hell were nipping at his heels, leaving her with the distinct impression he couldn't see the back of her fast enough.

She wondered what he and Braydon had been talking about. For all she knew, Braydon had warned him to stay away from her.

She had nearly reached the Woman's Institute and the library when her way was blocked by a menacing-looking man who seemed vaguely familiar. Nervously she glanced around, but no one else was within earshot.

"Mr. Hawkes sent me to tell you he needs to see you out at the ranch house immediately."

Lily drew herself up straight and tall. "Kindly tell Mr. Hawkes I'm not in the habit of dropping everything at his beck and call."

The man's dark, beady eyes bored into hers in an unsettling way. She got the distinct feeling there was something not quite right in the head about the fellow. He licked his lips, and a dribble of spittle found its way to his unshaven chin.

"I don't think Mr. Hawkes will be too happy with that message."

"Tell him I'll be by presently. At my convenience."

Lily turned and went inside the library. She opened her mouth to tell Rose where she was headed, then closed it abruptly. Rose wouldn't understand what she was playing at or why. Best to keep her in the dark.

She found her hat and gloves where she had left them earlier. "I'm going to head off now," she said with a fake cheerfulness in her voice, unsure if Rose even heard her. "I'll see you later."

At the livery she collected her borrowed horse and buggy. Hawkes had never summoned her this way before and for the first time ever she hoped that Barron had his eye on Hawkes's place. She'd feel better if someone knew where she was.

She sent a longing glance toward the hotel as she drove out of town. If only she could confide in Henrietta and Braydon about the charade she had entered into with Barron, their plan to take down Hawkes. It would be nice to have Henrietta and Braydon's support and backing. But Barron had insisted, in order for things to work as planned, it had to be a total surprise to the others. She knew he was right. She also knew there would be more than a little opposition if the family got wind of what they were up to.

# CHAPTER 7

"Looks like something's up, man." Secreted in their vantage point to watch Hawkes's ranch house, Benjamin passed Barron the spyglass.

Barron pressed his lips together in displeasure. He already knew what he would see, and while he had been taken aback by Lily's recent arrival at Hawkes's, he was royally ticked off that she hadn't mentioned it when they were together earlier at the hotel. What kind of partnership was it if they each kept things from the other?

One without a lot of mutual trust. He tuned out the little voice in his head that reminded him he hadn't always been forthcoming with Lily, either. He had his reasons.

Right now Lily rode from the barn alongside Hawkes, mounted on one of Hawkes's horses, and as he focused on her face up close, he saw she didn't look any happier with the arrangement than he was.

He passed the spyglass back to Ben. "I'm going to follow them."

"I'll come with you."

Barron shook his head. "It'll be that much harder for two

of us to tail them unnoticed. If, for some reason, I don't make it back in a few hours, come look for me."

Barron could tell Ben didn't like this latest development. For that matter, neither did he. But he couldn't leave Lily to ride off into the yonder, alone and unarmed, with Hawkes.

As Barron anticipated, the duo cut through from Hawkes's ranch to the rear of the old Ross place which eventually took them onto Copper Moon land. From there they followed the river and climbed steadily up toward the cliffs where, not long ago, Hawkes had tried to kill Laura.

Barron followed from a distance, barely close enough to keep them in sight and definitely out of firing range. What if Hawkes planned to force an unsuspecting Lily over the edge and into the gorge below?

"Damn woman is too trusting for her own good," he muttered under his breath. What had Lily been thinking when she started this charade? She knew squat about the realities of mounting a crusade to rid the world of evil louts like her old man. He and the rest of the Masons had been biding their time for years, yet Lily thought she could just waltz in where angels feared to tread.

Lily had precious little experience when it came to dealing with someone rotten clear through like Hawkes. Someone who held human life in such low regard.

He felt a slight wave of relief when, after some time in the saddle, the duo veered away from the cliffs. The direction they now headed was wide open, mostly desert, with little in the way of cover. Barely visible in the distance was the steep climb to where a series of caves held centuries-old secrets.

Barron didn't like this new destination any better. Wasn't it in one of the caves ahead that the now-dead newspaper reporter had discovered a cache of human remains? The fellow had guided Brody and Braydon to his findings, but whatever the reporter had seen had mysteriously disappeared by the time the three of them got back there. Shortly afterward, the reporter wound up dead.

Barron shook his head. He hated feeling that someone was always one step ahead of them. Which is precisely why no one other than Bishop knew about his plan with Lily. Not even Benjamin was in the know.

As the cover thinned to nothing, he was forced to dismount and continue on foot. Up ahead, he could see Hawkes and Lily clear as day, which meant all they had to do was look back and catch sight of him just as easily. He squatted low to the ground and prayed they kept their eyes forward.

RIDING ALONGSIDE HAWKES, Lily was hot and uncomfortable. She wasn't exactly dressed for this outing. Plus, the horse she rode was bigger than she was used to, as was the saddle. She slid a sideways look at her companion. Impossible to figure the man out. Somedays Hawkes passed himself off as affable and good natured. Other days he was, by turns, surly and taciturn. Today he had been positively animated, almost excited as he brushed aside her protests, insisting he had something of the utmost importance to show her.

Reluctantly she'd watched a groom saddle up one of the ranch nags before he'd helped her into the saddle, for she had no desire to accompany Hawkes into the back of beyond. As the miles passed, she suspected they had passed onto Copper Moon land but didn't know for sure.

Eventually Hawkes stopped and dismounted with a grunt, indicating she do the same.

Warily she eyed the rifle he pulled from across his saddle. "Are we anticipating trouble?"

"Never can tell," Hawkes said.

Lily wished she still had the pistol Barron had tucked into her hand that night after the wedding.

"This way," Hawkes said.

Lily glanced down at her fancy, high-button day boots, not exactly built to clamber her way up the side of a cliff. She shaded her eyes as she looked up to the yawning dark shadow of the opening to a cave.

"I wish you'd tell me what this is all about."

"A little show of faith, my dear," Hawkes said. "Once you see what I'm about to share with you, you'll realize the importance of me receiving the first installment of that money from your pa."

So that's what this was about! She should have known.

"I told you already, the money's not exactly at my fingertips. I may need to make a special trip out East to the solicitor and find out what's happening with Daddy's estate."

"I predict, once you lay eyes on what I'm about to show you, you'll be on your way post-haste."

"First things first," Lily said. "I'm still working on Barron to ensure the ranch's deed passes from Brody to him and then to you. The solicitor is unlikely to release any funds until I prove we can access the copper and open a mine, as per Daddy's last wishes."

Hawkes ignored her as he plowed his way forward on foot, grunting and puffing with every step up the switchback trail.

After what seemed like forever, they reached the mouth of the cave. Lily was a little alarmed by the bright red color of Hawkes's face. His shirt was dripping with sweat and even though they had stopped a few times along the way, he appeared to be having difficulty breathing.

"This way. Over here." He pushed her inside the cave where it was cool and dim, then stopped in his tracks and scratched his jaw as he stared at the rough stone of the inside wall. The cave was barely tall enough to stand in.

"Over here what?" Lily peered through the dim light but didn't see a thing.

"It was right over here." Hawkes pointed with his stubby finger, as if he expected whatever had gone missing might magically reappear. "This is where the assayer got his findings for the report I showed you."

"You're sure this is the right cave?" she asked. "Maybe one of the others—"

"This is the place." Hawkes's voice rang with certainty.

"This is where the assayer found evidence of copper?"

"Sure as I'm standing here."

Lily crossed her arms over her chest. "It looks like a whole lot of nothing to me."

He glowered at her. "You don't know squat. What was I thinking? Partnering with a woman."

"Perhaps you were thinking you'd run out of other options."

"You been listening too much to them ignorant Masons." As he spoke Hawkes tensed, straightened and edged sideways toward the entrance to the cave, keeping her in his sights.

Lily followed. She didn't like the way this day was shaping up.

"Son of a—" The second Hawkes stepped from the cave he released the safety on his rifle and aimed down below, near where they left the horses.

She followed his gaze to where Barron, out in the open and low to the ground, headed their way. He'd followed them! Her heart gave a crazy, happy hiccup. She wasn't out here alone with despicable Hawkes!

She watched in horror as Hawkes raised his rifle to rest on his shoulder. "What are you doing?"

"Taking down a right pesky Mason."

"That's Barron!" she shrieked. "He's alone. We need him."

Hawkes just growled low in his throat, a barely human sound. "There's no such thing as only one Mason. They're like a pack of fleas."

Lily stumbled toward Hawkes. If Barron got shot it would be all her fault. Besides which—

She reached out, no thought in her head other than to distract Hawkes and throw off his aim. He swatted her away with one hand, then lost his footing right before the gun discharged.

A searing heat burned through her upper left arm. She dropped to her knees cradling her injured arm, sucking in her breath as pain burned through her. She stared up at Hawkes in disbelief.

His mouth hung open. "I didn't mean ... You shouldn't ..."

From below, an answering shot whizzed past Hawkes's head.

"Damn it!" he roared. Brandishing his rifle like a crazy man, he took off in a different direction, leaving Lily to stare at the rapidly spreading splotch of red on her borrowed silk jacket. Just before she fainted.

～

SHE CAME to with a start as a damp cloth was pressed to her forehead. Her arm throbbed something fierce. She was lying on a hard-packed dirt floor. As her vision cleared she made out the shadowy stone walls of the cave behind an upside-down Barron, who sat behind her, frowning concern on his handsome face. Her head was pillowed on something hard, which turned out to be Barron's leg. She could feel him running an unsteady hand through her hair.

"Hawkes," she said through dry lips.

"Took off," Barron said.

"A bully *and* a coward." Carefully she turned her head toward the source of pain. She caught her breath when she saw the sleeve of her jacket had been cut away, her exposed arm bound in a chunk of cloth that must have stopped the bleeding. "I've never been shot before. Hurts like the dickens."

"I'll make you a sling," Barron said. "Usually Bishop is the one patching folks up, but I did my best. You were lucky. The bullet barely nicked you."

"Since when is getting shot considered lucky?"

"There's shot, and then there's shot dead. Still alive is lucky."

"You followed me," she said.

"Darn right. I wasn't about to sit back while you took off with Hawkes. Do you know why he brought you here?"

"He said this is where they were testing for copper. He appeared quite put out that all evidence of the assayer's tests had disappeared."

"When Bishop and I were out near here last week, someone took a shot at us. I figured it for Hawkes or one of his thugs." He gave her a long, level look. "Be interesting if it was someone else."

Lily considered his words. "Could there be someone who knows about the copper but is trying to cover it up?"

"We won't worry about that now. Do you feel like trying to sit up?"

At her nod, he placed a supportive arm under her back and slowly raised her to a seated position. She winced at the fresh wave of pain. "Can I please have a drink?"

"Sip slowly. There's not much left. I used most of it cleaning you up." He placed his canteen near her lips and she obediently parted her lips. The water was somewhat warm but still tasted marvelous.

He unsheathed his knife. "Sorry to be hacking at your pretty gown, but I need a chunk of fabric to make you a sling. It'll help ease the ache in your arm to have it supported."

"Go ahead." Lily gave up wondering how she might repair the damaged outfit before she returned it to its owner.

"Shame to ruin this silk. The color matches your eyes."

She gave an exaggerated flutter of her lashes. "Why Barron, what a romantic thing to say."

He shot her a rueful smile. "Not every day a lady tries to save my life and ends up getting shot for her trouble. Why did you throw yourself in the way to save me?"

Lily bit down on her bottom lip. The answer to that question was too troubling to contemplate. It might mean she was starting to have feelings for Barron. "I'd say this makes us even for any difficulty I caused you at the outset."

He leaned close. His warm breath fanned her cheeks. "I dunno about that. I'd say you still owe me."

"You would."

His mouth hovered inches from hers before he pulled

back, as if suddenly realizing how close he'd been to kissing her.

He cleared his throat. "About that sling. How about I save your skirt and use your petticoat instead?"

"Best then if I take it right off."

"I'll get it."

Barron's eyes never left hers as he reached up under her skirt, past her knees and over her hips. There was something shockingly intimate about a man with a hand up your skirt. She felt his fingers at her waist seeking the elastic band of the undergarment. Fingers slipped beneath the fabric, brushing bare skin. His breath caught. As did hers.

He pulled back as if burned. "You better do it."

"I don't think I can manage with only one hand."

His breath whistled between his tightly clamped teeth. It was amusing to see him so discomfited. She patted his arm with her good hand. "It's okay, Barron. I trust you."

He took hold of her petticoat, fumbling it down past her hips. "I never thought I'd hear you say that."

"If I didn't know better, I'd think you've never undressed a woman before."

"Damn it, Lily." He gave a final tug and the garment tumbled free. "You have no business saying things like that."

"Things like what?"

His mouth against hers, he spoke against her lips. "Things that make me crazy." Then he kissed her.

*She'd wanted this!*

Lily curled her good arm around his neck, her fingers tangled in his hair where it brushed the back of his collar, aware she had deliberately goaded him until he lost control.

Because if he didn't have control, it meant she did. And when it came to Barron, she liked having control.

A control that was solely tested as his hungry mouth

shaped and re-shaped hers. Took, tested, tasted, and came back for more.

The kiss went from rough to gentle, then back to rough before he pulled himself away, a man in conflict. He lurched to his feet and slashed her petticoat with his knife, cutting away the elastic and forming a misshapen square, which he folded into a triangle.

With great care, he squatted next to her and fashioned the makeshift sling so her arm was cradled against her ribs. She shivered as his fingers brushed the back of her neck while he tied a knot to hold it tight.

"That should do till we get back." He stood again and scooped up his canteen. "I'm going to go get some water for the return trip." Then he was gone, leaving her to stare after him, her fingers resting against her lips. Lips that still throbbed and felt swollen, yet strangely bereft without the pressure of his against them.

BENJAMIN HAD no idea how long he remained in the twins' secret observation spot from which Hawkes's driveway, stables and front door were all in full view. He wished Barron would show up. How long was he supposed to wait until he sounded the alarm and organized a search?

He was just getting ready to make a move when he spotted Hawkes. The man was alone, two riderless horses in tow, a bad sign if there ever was one. Ben waited until Hawkes disappeared inside the barn, then took off for the Copper Moon.

He found Bishop down at the river getting washed up. None of the others were around. He didn't mince words. "Barron's missing. Likely Lily as well."

Bishop froze. "Missing how?"

"He and I were watching Hawkes's place. You know the spot."

Bishop nodded.

"Lily showed up at the house, which Barron found odd because he'd just seen her in town and she hadn't mentioned a word about any meeting planned with Hawkes. Next thing we knew, the two of them had mounted up and were riding off."

"Let me guess. Barron followed them."

Benjamin nodded grimly. "He insisted on going alone."

Bishop headed for his horse. "Sounds like Barron."

"I saw Hawkes come back with two other horses. One of them belongs to Barron."

Bishop blew out a breath. "Any idea which direction they took? Barron would have marked a trail we could follow in case something like this happened."

"All I know is they started toward the old Ross place. From there it's anyone's guess."

"What was Barron wearing?"

"White shirt, brown vest. Why?"

Bishop turned in the direction of the ranch house and the cabins. "Luckily, Rose is still in town. I'll go get changed."

Benjamin frowned. "What are you getting changed for?"

"I'll go over to Hawkes's and pretend I'm Barron. Given what you just said, he won't be expecting me. If we're lucky, he'll blurt out something that will help narrow the search."

"What about Brody and the others?" Benjamin asked.

"Best we try and handle this on our own."

"Well, hurry up. It's not long until dark."

BARRON BURST out of the cave and sucked a big lungful of air. He ran a hand through his hair and plopped his hat back onto his head. Lily would be okay for a spell while he went to check on his horse. But when he got to where he'd secured it, his horse was nowhere in sight. He let out a whistle but received no answering whinny. Hawkes must have taken him. Which likely meant he'd rounded up Lily's mount as well.

He stared off into the distance. Had Hawkes taken off in order to come back with reinforcements? The man never played fair. Two against one wouldn't have suited him.

He concentrated on trying to figure out how Hawkes's mind worked, anticipate the killer's next move, but it was impossible. There was no telling what the man might do if he believed he'd burned his bridges by shooting Lily.

Barron made his way downriver to a spot where he could clamber over the rocks to the water's edge. The river rushed by, reminding him of the time Laura had jumped in to save herself from Hawkes. Brody had followed her in an effort to save his love, even though he couldn't swim.

How was one supposed to know? What must it be like to feel such love for another human being that you'd sacrifice your own life for that of your love? Behind him Lily lay bleeding, having taken a bullet intended for him. He turned to go back.

Not only that, she'd all but begged him to kiss her. He brushed aside the memory of her sweet lips beneath his. She didn't really want him to kiss her. Her reaction was more like suddenly feeling close to death, and reaching out to embrace whatever life offered.

She was his responsibility. He had to get her out of here safely and back to town before he sent her on her way. Hawkes was too unpredictable for a sweet thing like Lily to tangle with, his actions getting worse the more desperate he became.

Barron stooped to refill his canteen, replaced the cork and started to rise, only to hear a distressing pop from behind his knee cap, followed by a gut-wrenching pain.

# CHAPTER 8

Lily was alarmed when Barron returned limping heavily and leaning on a decrepit stick. "What happened to you?"

"Wrenched something I shouldn't have. Old fight injury that flares up every once in a while when I move it wrong."

Lily worried her bottom lip. "Can you ride?"

He gave her an unsettling look. "Wouldn't matter any if I could or couldn't."

"What do you mean?"

"Your friend Hawkes made off with our horses."

"Hardly my friend. He shot me." Lily made her way gingerly to her feet, favoring her injured arm. "We should get started. It's a long trek on foot."

Barron gave her another telling look. "Neither of us is in any shape to be heading off on foot. Move too much and you'll start bleeding again. Plus, it'll be dark soon. Best we just hunker down and wait for help."

"No one knows where we are," she said in dismay.

"Ben knows I was tailing you. When I don't make it back by dark, he'll gather up the others and come after us."

"It's a huge area. We could be stranded here for days."

"Doubt it," Barron said shortly. "Bishop will know to look for a marked trail." At her questioning look he added, "It's an old habit from when we were young and one of us went off someplace without the other. Meanwhile, I'll go gather up some dry brush and stuff to start a fire."

"Shouldn't you be resting your bad leg?"

"I will once I get a fire started. Whoever comes will be looking out for smoke. Besides, it cools down in the evenings."

"What if Hawkes comes back with some of his thugs?"

Barron sent her a look she was unable to read.

"I'll protect you. What's the matter? You worried about being alone with me out here?"

*Alone.* How did she feel about the thought of the two of them possibly stranded overnight?

"Why don't you grab up what's left of your petticoat? I'll use it as a sack to carry the stuff for the fire." He started to take a step forward but his knee collapsed and he went down with a grimace of pain.

Lily gave him a sympathetic look. "Best you wait here. I'll go see what I can gather up."

He rolled to one side, leaned on the stick and pulled himself back to his feet with difficulty. "I don't want you out there by yourself."

"You're in no position to argue," she pointed out. "I can't exactly help you up if you take a tumble. I promise I'll stay in sight. You'll be more use to both of us if you rest that leg so we can get out of here."

She could tell he wasn't used to having a woman tell him what to do and didn't much like it. He opened his mouth as if to argue, then closed it. "Stay in sight then." He unholstered his gun as he spoke.

She eyed the gun in his hand. "What's that for?"

"In case."

"In case what?"

Barron shrugged. "Wild animals. Hawkes and his thugs sneaking back to finish us off. Take your pick."

Lily figured it was pretty much the same, Hawkes being no better than a wild animal. But she kept her thoughts to herself

It proved slow going to reach flat ground, and every movement jostled her arm, bringing a fresh wave of pain. She'd longed for adventure, she reminded herself. She'd certainly found it here in Bullet. At least she and Barron had moved past the stage of spitting daggers at each other. Wouldn't it be interesting to see how the others received news of the two of them being stranded together?

Benjamin heaved a sigh of relief when Bishop emerged unscathed from Hawkes's ranch house. He rode over to meet him away from the house and its occupants.

Bishop wore a huge grin. "Man acted like he'd seen a ghost. Especially when I asked why he took off with my horse. Started rambling about how the whole thing had been an accident. He didn't mean to shoot Miss Lilith. I had to act surprised, like I had no idea Lily had been with him."

"He shot Lily?"

"Sounds that way. Said he spotted me, tripped, and the gun went off accidentally. Blathered on about how he hoped this misunderstanding didn't affect the business arrangement between the three of us. I didn't have to put on an act to come off as all pissed. I asked him how he could just leave Lily behind."

"Let's just hope she's okay," Ben said darkly, fingers tightening instinctively on the barrel of his rifle. "The man has a habit of leaving dead bodies in his wake."

"Barron will take care of her. I have a feeling he cares for her more than he lets on."

"You believe that?"

"Stranger things have happened," Bishop said. "Hawkes claims he came back to get help. That he was planning to go fetch Doc Parsons."

"That I'll believe when I see it."

"He was well into his cups when I got there. Didn't appear to be in any hurry to go fetch the doc."

"Did he happen to mention where this went down?"

"I gather from what he said that it was up near the caves."

"Those wretched caves." Ben swore. "What is the big fascination?"

"I don't know. But it's high time we found out." As if by unspoken agreement, they both urged their horses to a gallop. "Let's hope Lily knows the answer to that when we get to her and Barron."

"Shouldn't we tell the others?" Ben asked.

"I vote we hold off for now," Bishop said. "Barron and Lily are working on a scheme to trip up Hawkes. No one else knows about it, and it might be better if it stays that way."

Ben pulled up short. "I thought we were done with secrets in this family."

Bishop barked out a laugh.

"I don't suppose you're in the know regarding this so-called arrangement Hawkes mentioned?"

"Not exactly. But it's unlikely Brody will be best pleased once he finds out."

"I don't like the sound of that, divided family loyalties, even if Barron thinks he's doing the right thing."

"I know," Bishop said. "I've been wrestling with it myself."

"As we all know," Ben said, "nothing goes on hereabouts that Brody doesn't eventually find out about. Can you still follow Barron's trail once we lose the light?"

"I sure hope so."

BARRON LEANED HEAVILY against the wall at the opening of the cave trying to take some of the weight off his bum leg. Of all times for it to give way! He knew that by tomorrow the leg should be, if not right as rain, settled down enough to move around on more easily.

True to her word, Lily stayed in view except for a few short moments when she disappeared behind a boulder. He was going to call out and tell her to get back out there, then realized she was likely attending to private matters. She was back in sight in relatively short order, and looked his way from time to time to give him an all-clear wave with her good arm.

She'd abandoned the trashed petticoat, electing to load her skirt with twigs and grasses till it ballooned full, clutching it closed with both hands. Holding her skirt that way had to hurt like hell. Clearly, she was a lot tougher than she looked.

Eventually she started the climb back toward him. With her skirt bunched up into a carry sack, her pantalettes helped preserve her modesty.

He gave his head a shake. What was he thinking, trying

to ogle a glimpse of Lily's underpinnings? Except he couldn't erase the memory of sliding his hands up there earlier, grazing the soft skin near her middle. He was pretty sure his touch had affected her as much as it affected him. Hadn't she all but begged him to kiss her?

He hobbled over to meet her.

"This okay?" she asked anxiously. She let go of her skirt hem and the bits and pieces tumbled to the ground.

"You did good," he told her. Gingerly he bent over and brushed at the front of her skirt to make sure there were no thorns or slivers to attack her. He straightened and almost fell but she grabbed him with her good arm, and he steadied them both as they ended up in each other's arms.

"Aren't we the pair?" she said with a half laugh.

He silenced her with his fingertips on her lips before he gathered her close and simply held her. He took a deep breath, savoring the fresh, floral fragrance of her hair. His heart jerked in a staccato beat. His breathing was erratic—fast, then slow, then speeded up again.

She felt so good in his arms, so right. As if he'd finally found the part of him that had been missing his entire life. He rested his cheek against the top of her head. He knew she was tough, but she felt so fragile, he wanted nothing more than to protect her and keep her safe.

"Are you okay?" Her words were muffled against the front of his shirt.

"Yeah." Reluctantly he released her. "We'd better get this fire started."

"You're sure they'll come after us?"

"Trust me. They'll be along." Even as he spoke, he felt a pang of regret. What might it have been like to spend the night out here with her, forced to huddle together for warmth as the night air grew cool? He half-wished their rescuers would wait until the next day.

"You must be tired of standing," she said, once the fire was lit and the flames caught. "Let me help you get comfortable."

He opened his mouth in protest, then closed it again. He wasn't used to accepting help from anyone, let alone a woman. "Sure. Thanks."

Once she helped him stretch out, close enough to feed bits and pieces to the fire as needed, she positioned herself next to him with their shoulders brushing. He didn't even think about it, just reached for her as if it was the most natural thing in the world, and pulled her close. She nuzzled against him trustingly, like the cat they used to have at the ranch, and closed her eyes.

"I'm hungry," she said in a tiny voice.

Barron reached into his vest pocket and pulled out a piece of hardtack. "This is all I've got."

"Thank you." She took the dry biscuit, broke it in half and passed him the biggest piece.

He shook his head. "It's for you."

He recognized that stubborn expression. "I'll only eat if you will."

"Have you always been this difficult?"

"No, but I'm quickly learning from the best."

He bit back a smile and accepted a chunk of biscuit, surprised how good it felt to provide for Lily as they munched together in companionable silence, washing the dry biscuit down with sips of water. Barron knew his canteen of water wouldn't last forever. But for now, the lady at his side had enough to sustain her.

~

CRADLED AGAINST BARRON, Lily experienced a myriad of conflicting emotions. He'd been so kind and tender toward her, even in a difficult situation. She had total confidence in his assurance that they would be rescued soon. With Barron by her side, she felt as if nothing bad would happen to her ever again. When had their animosity been replaced by this warm, caring companionship?

"I hope what happened today hasn't wrecked things with Hawkes. He knows he shot me."

"I'm pretty sure he knows you're his only hope. I wager if you show up, all sweet and forgiving, say you know it was an accident then sweeten the pot with the first installment of your loan to him, he'll fall into your lap."

She made a face. "Last place I want him."

"Figure of speech," Barron said. "We'll give him just enough line to grab the hook, then reel him in."

"We'll need to tell Brody what we're up to," she said.

"I agree. It's time to move the plan forward. You said Hawkes can't read much, right?"

"He can read some simple words. But nothing too complicated."

Barron nodded. "That ought to be perfect to help implement what I'm thinking we should do next."

"What's that?"

"You can tell Hawkes that Brody insists we get married due to us being stranded out here. Brody pulled the same move on Bradley last year when he thought Bradley had put Amanda in a compromising position. The whole town knows their story, so it's highly believable Brody would make the same decree to you and me."

Lily nodded, her mind racing, anxious to see this all in the past. "If we were to plan the 'fake wedding' for a week or two from now, do we have time to line everything up?"

"I don't see why not. You tell Hawkes there's no point in waiting; it's your chance to get the deed. Tell him he's the closest thing you have to a male relative to give you away and that it's what your daddy would have wanted from your new business partner. Don't forget, he'll be feeling flush from the first of the monies you're going to front him. I bet he'll do anything to ingratiate you if it brings him more cash."

Lily caught his enthusiasm. "I can tell him I always wanted an outdoor wedding on a ranch. I'll insist on inviting the whole town because we need their blessing. Not just for you and me, but for the new venture in mining. If everyone shows up, Hawkes will believe that with my help and fortune, he has regained the respect of the entire town. We both know he'll waste no time abusing their trust with more bullying and exploitation."

"And everyone will be on hand when the Masons deliver the blow that destroys Hawkes."

Lily pressed her lips together thoughtfully. "Will you kill him?" Not that she felt Hawkes deserved mercy, but she couldn't sanction the killing of another human being, even though she knew Hawkes had killed time and again.

Barron didn't quite meet her gaze. "Either the law will take care of him or we will. Maybe both."

HAWKES PACED his den in a restless circle. He should have known better than to have Denim dispose of those bones. He couldn't risk having a weak link. Not when everything he had worked for his entire life was nearly within reach. His for the taking.

Denim needed to be disposed of before he ruined

Hawkes's plans. Prosperity from the copper. Control of the entire territory, starting with Bullet and branching out from there. More wealth than he could spend in one lifetime. Maybe even a powerful government position. All the respect he was due. Yes indeed. Best he see Denim taken care of. Discreetly.

BRODY AND BRAYDON rode into the barn, dismounted and started to unsaddle their horses in companionable silence. All of a sudden they heard a thud from an empty stall. Without a word, their eyes met in silent communication as they unholstered their guns.

"Who's there?" Brody barked.

Silence.

"I suggest you put your hands in the air where we can see them and make yourself visible before we fill you full of lead," Braydon said.

Two hands shot into view above the wall of the stall. "Don't shoot!" Slowly a man moved into sight.

"You alone?" Brody asked.

The man nodded.

"Come out slow," Brody said. "No sudden moves."

Brody didn't recognize the man who shuffled forward, licking his lips nervously. Braydon stepped forward and relieved the stranger of his gun.

"Talk!" Braydon said, his pistol aimed straight for the fellow's chest.

"I know stuff," the man said. "Stuff about Hawkes no one else knows."

"Why would we care?" Braydon said.

"Everyone hereabouts knows you all are sworn enemies."

Braydon half-turned to Brody. "I sense a trap. How about you, Brody? Strikes me as funny some thug of Hawkes's would show up offering to spill the goods on his boss."

"I know too much. He's planning to kill me once he finds me. But he won't think to look here."

"Why should we believe you?" Brody said.

"Those bones the reporter fella found? I know where they are. I'll take you to them."

Brody subjected the man to a long, searching glance before he exchanged looks with Braydon. "I think you're right. It looks like a setup to get us out where Hawkes can plan another dynamite ambush."

Bradley arrived in the barn, took one look at the intruder and pulled his own weapon. "What's he doing here?"

"You know him?" Braydon asked.

Bradley's face darkened. "Sure do."

"This the guy who beat you the time Hawkes grabbed you up?"

Bradley nodded.

"Says he wants to switch sides against Hawkes," Brody said.

"That so?" Bradley addressed the intruder. "Are you prepared to tell what you know to the law? Everything you know about Hawkes?"

The fellow nodded. "Long as I get protection from Hawkes."

"What do you boys think?" Brody asked the other two. "Could it be we just got handed the final nail in Hawkes's coffin?"

The other two nodded.

"I am pretty sure the marshal will be very interested in what our friend here has to say," Brody said. "We just need to make sure we stash him someplace Hawkes won't get to him first."

# CHAPTER 9

As darkness closed in around them, Barron felt Lily give a little shiver and move closer to him as he fed more dried brush into their fire. At the same time, he cast a vigilant eye out to the desert, hoping the flames didn't attract unwanted creatures.

"Are there wild animals out there?" Lily asked.

He tensed. Uncanny, the way she seemed to read his thoughts.

"More than likely," he said gruffly. It was good to remember that once the curtain came down on their little charade, Lily would be moving on. She'd likely get a charge from her role in helping take Hawkes down. None of his business what she did after that.

"What do you think might happen? Once this is all behind us, I mean." She was doing it again!

How was he supposed to know what he'd do next? For the many years he'd been focused on avenging his older brother's death, he'd missed out on the joys of everyday life here that the others seemed to have found. Like Bradley had discovered through fatherhood. And Brody with creating and nurturing their extended family. Blake, helping Storm with the book wagon. Not to mention Braydon, working alongside Henrietta to oversee construction of the hotel in town.

"I guess you'll go back out on the trail," she said when he didn't respond.

He didn't feel like telling her what Brody had said about the cattle drives eventually coming to an end. Thoughts of returning to his earlier con-artist ways, bilking unsuspecting folk in a rigged game didn't hold much appeal. Especially a solo gig without Bishop. Bishop, who'd been with him every step of the way until now, would likely start his own family once Hawkes was no longer a threat.

If Lily was hoping he'd ask her what she planned to do, he wasn't taking the bait.

"Is the fire likely to attract the animals?" she asked.

Barron hoped not. "Nah! I've been many a night on the trail where one of us stays awake to make sure the fire didn't go out."

"That's good." As she spoke, Lily nestled closer. As he watched her struggle to keep her eyes open, she seemed fragile, vulnerable, in need of his protection more than ever. Or was it because she wasn't jawing off at him in her usual snippy fashion?

*That* Lily was a lot easier to keep at arm's length.

"Go ahead," he said. "Close your eyes for a few minutes. I'll look after things." It struck him as he spoke that he'd never before felt the sole responsibility for another human being in quite the same way. Sure, he'd felt responsible for Bishop, but they were equals. And Joe had been so much older. His big brother had been the one to look out for them, not the opposite. Having Lily curled up next to him all trusting and innocent was a new experience. One that stirred him in unsettling ways as he stared from the flames into the darkness beyond.

He could tell from her even breathing that Lily had fallen asleep and wished the others would hurry and find them, even as he wished he could prolong this time alone with her. His musings were interrupted by a long, low recognizable whistle. Bishop!

Lily stirred and blinked awake as he whistled back, letting Bishop know they were alone and all right. He sensed movement below, but couldn't make out how many riders were there.

"What is it?" Lily asked sleepily.

"Our ticket out of here."

Did he just imagine he heard her say, "That's too bad"?

He squinted into the darkness but there was no further sign of movement, no other sound. His gut clenched. He tried to rise, but didn't want to disturb Lily who seemed so cozy. This would be his last chance to be this close to her. He pulled her close, his protective instincts on high alert.

"Bishop," he called to his twin. "Where are you?"

"Over here!"

Barron started and turned to see Bishop appear behind them. He'd come up the back trail to the ledge out front, the same way Hawkes had run off.

As Bishop moved into the light his gaze shifted from Barron to Lily curled against him, then back to Barron, eyebrows raised in a silent question that Barron chose to ignore.

"Who's down there?" Barron indicated the area below with a movement of his head.

"Ben's there with the horses. We figured we'd make sure you were alone before we showed ourselves." His gaze homed in on Barron. "You're sitting funny. I told Ben I figured your knee must have gone out when you stayed here instead of coming down to us."

Bishop advanced and reached down a hand to pull Barron to his feet before he turned to Lily. "You okay?" he asked her. "I heard Hawkes shot you."

"He didn't mean to."

"How'd you know that?" Barron asked, feeling the circulation slowly return to his legs. He shifted from foot to foot as the familiar pins and needles sensation from sitting still too long worked its way through.

"Simple. I pretended to be you. All pissed off that Hawkes took my horse."

Barron nodded. "I shoulda guessed."

"Fastest way to track you down. Your trail-marking skills are a little rusty," Bishop added.

"Says who? I'm thinking marriage has made you soft," Barron countered.

Lily stood and dusted her skirt with her free hand. "Are you two going to stand here all night exchanging pleasantries or put out this fire and take us home?"

Something about the way she said home tugged further at Barron's gut. Did she mean the ranch? Could the Copper Moon be starting to feel like home to her?

"Give Lily a hand. I'm okay," he said gruffly.

"Bishop, ignore your stubborn brother. I've been up and down from here on my own just fine. He's the one who needs a hand." Lily flounced off toward where Benjamin waited with the horses, leaving the two of them to douse the fire.

Bishop gave him one of those looks he choose to ignore, as he emptied part of his canteen on the fire. "What's going on here, bro?"

"Nothing," Barron said. "Let's get going."

THE FOLLOWING DAY, Rose accompanied Lily to Doc Parson's office, where he cleaned and rebandaged her injury.

"Not a bad stitching job," he said as he inspected Bishop's first aid efforts from the previous evening after they returned to the ranch house. He straightened up and washed his hands. "You were lucky, young lady. Your arm should heal up right as rain. But I suggest in the future you stay away from loaded firearms. How'd you say you got shot?"

Lily heaved a sigh. "Just in the wrong place at the wrong time. How long do I need to wear the sling?"

"I'd give it a week, just to keep the arm stable. There shouldn't be any permanent damage to the muscle."

Lily cocked a look at her sister. "That's good. We have a lot to do. A wedding to plan. I certainly hope you and the missus are able to join us."

"Let me guess," the doc said. "Another one of them Mason fellows doing the deed?"

"That's right," Lily said brightly. "My sis... My future sister-in-law, Miss Rose, has agreed to stand up with me." It was getting harder all the time to keep up the façade that Lily was a wealthy heiress recently arrived in town, and no kin to Rose. But in order to set the stage to take down Hawkes, no one in town could know the truth.

"I wish you luck, young lady. Both of you," he added. "Those Mason boys have always been a handful. Was after thinking a woman's steadying influence would be a good thing, but all the wives seem to have their own ideas as to how things ought to be done around here, and the fellows can't seem to rein 'em in. My wife knows her place is in our home, and that's for sure. Too much change, ladies running around building town halls and hotels, is bad for the town and those in it."

Lily exchanged a look with Rose. The doctor had no idea of the changes looming ahead. "Thanks, Doc." She hopped down off the examination table. "See you in a couple of weeks."

"Where's the wedding?" the doctor asked.

Lily smiled. "He doesn't know it yet, but Mr. Hawkes will be hosting the ceremony and giving me away."

"Guy Hawkes!" The doctor let out a snort of disbelief. "I'd pay good money to be there and see that. The Mason brothers, guests of honor at the home of their enemy. Yes indeed. Wouldn't miss it for the world." He gave Lily an approving look. "Maybe you'll prove a good influence after all, miss."

BRODY GAVE BARRON A QUESTIONING LOOK. "Let me get this straight. You want me to announce I'm forcing you to marry Lily, on account of you two were stranded together for a couple of hours?"

"Sounds stupid," Braydon said.

"No one will believe it," Bradley added.

Barron's gaze moved around the kitchen table, not sensing a lot of support from the men gathered there, not even his twin.

"We're not going to really get married," he said. "We're just going to stage a wedding with everyone there." He sought Brody's eyes. "You said yourself we're ready to finish what we started with Hawkes. This gives us the perfect opportunity."

"It's too dangerous," Brody said.

"Lily knows what she's getting herself into."

"It's not just Lily, it's our wives and children." He gave Barron a disappointed look. "I know you're used to fighting yourself out of any situation

but this involves more than just you. You and Lily had no business going off half-cocked and hatching some cocka-mamie scheme between the two of you. And I'll tell her so myself next time I see her."

"There's more," Barron said in a rush. "Lily started this all by herself. Enlisted Zara's help to put it together. She's got some wild idea about helping make amends for all the evil her father imposed on others by taking Hawkes down."

"That's crazy," Benjamin said.

"I thought so too. But we've come this far."

"Tell her to drop it. To hightail it far, far away where Hawkes will never find her."

Barron stood. "I'm not going to do that," he said slowly. "The plan is solid and it's going ahead, with or without the blessing of all of you here."

Brody blinked. A muscle clenched in the corner of his jaw. "You're that committed? You'd move forward even knowing the family was opposed?"

Barron felt a hollow emptiness echo inside of him. Maybe he did feel closer to everyone here than he'd real-ized. Maybe these men really were his family, his future tangled up with theirs.

"Isn't there some way we can come to an agreement? A way for us all to see what we started out to do together all those years ago to a satisfying conclusion."

The silence in the room was deafening. Barron swal-lowed thickly. He'd done it now. Isolated himself so far from the others there'd be no coming back. Slowly Brody rose and held out his hand. "I've been waiting a long time for this day."

*The day Brody and the rest of them got rid of him?*

Barron stood and slid his hand into Brody's as the others rose and gathered around. Was this their idea of a send-off? Would he even get a chance to say goodbye to the wives? The youngsters? His life felt hollow and empty. Lily's face swam in and out of focus. "I can't say it's unexpected."

"I've been expecting it for a long time," Brody said. "For you to finally realize you're truly with us, one of us. And that we work together. Welcome to the family! We've got Hawkes's right-hand man under wraps, just dying to spill what he knows. Should be more than enough to enlist the help of the law and see Hawkes finally gets what he has coming."

Lily and Rose hastened their steps as they passed the café. "I wish we could tell Georgina what's really going on," Rose said. "She's going to be hurt you didn't ask her to fix the food."

Lily gave her sister a serious look. "You and I both know there will be no after-wedding party. The less folks who know the truth, the better."

Rose nodded. "I need to head over to the library, since Storm is away in the book wagon. Where are you meeting Barron?"

"At the café. He's been around town complaining to anyone who will listen how Brody is forcing him to marry me because we got stranded together overnight."

"And the two of you are going to see Hawkes? Is that a good idea?"

"It's the only way. Bishop and Ben will be watching to make sure things go as planned."

Rose placed one hand softly against her sister's cheek. "It's hard to imagine where we'd be if you hadn't been kidnapped and I came after you." She swallowed thickly. "I confess I wish the wedding wasn't just a ruse to take down Hawkes. I wish you were really marrying Barron and staying here in Bullet."

"Don't be silly," Lily said quickly. "Barron and I can't stand each other." The words sounded hollow in her ears. Somewhere along the way her feelings for Barron had taken an unexpected turn. If only he felt the same. But after gaining the support of Brody and the family for their scheme, he seemed like a different man. He barely noticed her.

Rose shrugged. "I know Barron can be a pain. But I think that chip on his shoulder is mostly a cover-up to protect how much he's hurting inside. Bishop says Barron blames himself for Joe getting killed."

"It wasn't Barron's fault, was it?"

"Apparently Barron finds it easier to blame himself, than to blame his big brother for making wrong choices."

"You mean because Joe went to work for Hawkes?"

"Joe was trying to get rich quick so he could take care of his younger brothers. Once they caught up with him here, they begged him to join them at Brody's. And I think maybe that was his plan, except Hawkes got wind of it and killed him before he had the chance."

Lily nodded grimly. "Barron told me Hawkes killed Joe before the others realized what was happening and could intervene."

"Hawkes still wears Joe's knife on his belt, the one he took from Joe's body that night."

Lily shuddered. "I've seen that knife."

"I don't think any of the brothers will be truly at peace until they see the knife turned on Hawkes."

BARRON WAS WAITING for Lily near the café. He passed her a thick envelope. "This should be enough to bait the trap."

Lily took a quick look at the contents. "Where did you get all this cash?"

"Doesn't matter," Barron said shortly. "Let Hawkes think it was wired to you by your daddy's solicitor and you just picked it up from the bank over in Yuma where you are now doing business."

She gave him a cynical smile as she stashed the envelope in her reticule. "And I couldn't wait to rush over and give it to Hawkes as a symbol of forgiveness for him shooting me."

"Something like that." Barron helped her into her borrowed rig, swung in next to her and picked up the reins. "I'll be right outside while you go in and talk to Hawkes."

"What if he refuses to come out and talk to you? What if he suspects a trap?"

"Let's hope greed makes him stupid."

"Was it hard to get Brody and the others to go along with our plan?"

She felt the way he tensed at her words and knew him well enough to know she had broached a subject he'd rather not talk about.

"You'd think it was all their idea," he said finally. "But they took it one step further. It'll work good."

Lily nodded and filled the drive with chatter about their upcoming "fake nuptial" and what she and Rose planned to wear on the big day.

When they reached Hawkes's, she turned to Barron before she disembarked. "Is there any chance Hawkes knows Joe was your brother?"

Barron shook his head. "Bishop and I were headed this way to look for Joe when we first tangled with Brody all those years back. We didn't know till after that Joe was one ranch over from where we were staying with Brody and the others. Joe wouldn't have let on to Hawkes. Especially if he was thinking of allying with Brody and the rest against Hawkes."

Lily nodded. "Wish me luck."

"I have all the faith in the world in you."

Lily turned away before Barron saw how much his words meant. No one had ever expressed faith in her before.

HAWKES WAS MUTTERING to himself as he came from the bunkhouse. Still no sign of Denim, and none of the other hands seemed to know where the foreman had run off to. He ought to have taken care of Denim when he had the chance. He'd known the fellow was a powder keg waiting to explode, even though Denim couldn't spill anything he knew to the law without incriminating himself in the bargain.

Wherever Denim had lit out for, he'd been on foot, which ought to make him easy to track down. This time he'd make sure Denim's big mouth was silenced once and for all.

He came around the corner of the ranch house and stopped abruptly. Little Miss Lilith's rig was parked out front. She stood alongside it, looking up all dewy-eyed at the man holding the reins. One of them cursed Masons. On his property. He pulled his gun and started brandishing it as he approached.

Miss Lilith turned and gave him a chilly look. "Put that away before you shoot me again," she said. "I won't be so quick to forgive you a second time."

He noticed the sling, bright white against her grass-green fancy jacket, before he locked gazes with Mason. "Touch your gun and you're a corpse."

"I'm only here because she made me," Mason said.

Hawkes ignored him and turned to the chit. "Why's he here? Said all I needed to say to him the other day when he busted in."

"I wanted to let you know things are progressing nicely," she said. "Daddy's solicitor sent me the money I asked for. Meanwhile, Brody is insisting Barron make an honest woman out of me."

Maybe things really were looking up, Hawkes conceded, relaxing his grip on his pistol. "You got the money on you?"

"Of course," she said primly. "That was our original partnership arrangement. But things have changed."

He narrowed his gaze suspiciously. "What's changed?"

"It's high time you got respectable around here if you're going to be involved in a business venture with me. One that involves hiring the locals. Our wedding day should accomplish that nicely."

"How's that?" Hawkes licked his lips.

Miss Priss smiled and raised her eyes skyward. "I feel my daddy looking down and nodding, happy that you will be the one to give me away, since he's no longer with us."

"Me? Give away the bride?" Hawkes envisioned the townsfolk witnessing the first of many among his upcoming new triumphs. Respectability was a stepping stone into a government official's shoes. Then he frowned. "What about the deed to the ranch?"

Mason spoke up. "That's my worry. I'll be handing it over to Lily as a wedding gift. What she does with it after that..." He shrugged.

"You sound pretty sure of yourself," Hawkes said.

"Give him the money," Mason told the girl.

Hawkes felt Mason's gaze follow him as he grabbed the thick envelope she offered and thumbed the contents. His hand shook as he shoved the cash in his pants pocket. To think this was only the beginning. Plenty more where this came from.

"Would Lily be handing over such a generous first installment if she didn't have every confidence I can deliver the deed?"

"I hope you're not planning a long engagement," Hawkes said. "Once I have that deed in hand, the mining gets under way post haste."

"How's next week?" Lilith said sweetly. "I've always wanted to get married outdoors on a ranch."

Hawkes narrowed his gaze. "Whose ranch?" He'd be damned if he set foot again on Mason's spread until the place was officially his.

"Why right here, of course," she said. "The pond should make a perfect backdrop for the ceremony. We'll bring over benches and chairs from the hall. Set out a big spread afterward on the back terrace." She tilted her head as if studying him. "You'll need a nice custom-tailored suit."

"A suit?"

"Of course," she said. "Something befitting your new station in life."

# CHAPTER 10

Storm and Blake returned with the book wagon a few days later, and Lily wasted no time seeking out Storm to alter Rose's wedding dress for her to wear.

"Are you sure you wouldn't rather have a wedding dress of your own, instead of a hand-me-down?" Storm asked through a mouthful of straight pins as she pinned where to take the dress in at the waist and hips and let it out through the bosom. "I can make you one in plenty of time."

"Don't be silly," Lily said. "I mean, it's not like I'm really getting married."

"Right," Storm said as she crouched down to pin the hem. "There have been so many weddings lately that it's difficult to remember this one is all a pretense."

"Make that a trap," Lily said. "With Hawkes as the target."

Storm straightened. "I can't help but worry that something might go wrong."

Lily patted her arm reassuringly. "Nothing will go wrong. Hawkes will finally get what he deserves for all the death and misery he has caused, not just to the Masons but to the entire population around Bullet."

Storm bit her lower lip. "I hate to think of anymore killing."

Lily loosened the dress's fastenings and stepped out of it. "Who said anything about killing Hawkes? Brody is planning to publicly announce the man's financial ruin, right before he turns him over to the authorities."

"Hawkes is slippery. I guarantee he won't go easily." Storm gave Lily a long, level look. "He'll never forgive you for your part in this."

"Stop worrying. Hawkes will be behind bars, penniless. And I'll be in a different part of the country."

"Now that makes me sad," Storm said. "I wish Rose could persuade you to stay."

Lily shook her head. "Rose and I have been together our entire lives. It's past time we each made our own way. She loves it here."

"What about you?" Storm asked.

Lily pressed her lips together thoughtfully. There was much about Bullet and the Mason clan she found appealing. "I have a lot more adventures ahead of me, away from Bullet."

Storm tilted her head to one side. "I spent years on the run. Afraid of the man I had married. Equally afraid of the law if it turned out I had accidentally killed him."

Lily sniffed. "That horrid creature got what he deserved. From what you've said, he was a bullying tyrant who preyed on women and made their lives miserable." She thought of her father who preyed on anyone and everyone he could, all under the guise of salvation and eternal life. She and Rose were so lucky to have gotten away.

Storm opened and closed her mouth a few times, as if debating whether to speak. "It's not my place to say this."

Lily chuckled. "When has that ever stopped you?"

Storm gave an acknowledging half smile. "It strikes me there are many ways to help the victims of men like the one I was married to."

"What do you mean?"

"Someone could do a lot of good here in the west if there was someplace safe for women who find themselves in a similar situation to get away from their husbands. Someplace they could even take their kids without having to constantly look over their shoulder."

Lily gave Storm a searching look. "You've been giving this a lot of thought."

She sighed. "I see those women when I'm out with the book wagon. I recognize the defeated look in their eyes and the hopeless slump to their shoulders. I know what it's like to have no one and no place to go."

As Lily digested Storm's words, she acknowledged how lucky she was. As difficult as their early lives had been, she'd always had her sister. And when the chance came to escape, she hadn't hesitated, never doubting Rose would find her.

"The dress should look nice," Storm said as Lily passed it over. "I'll have it fixed up before you know it."

"I appreciate that," Lily said, happy to be back in her everyday clothing, even if the garments were only on loan.

Storm gathered up her sewing equipment. "I'm still surprised that Barron convinced Brody and the others to go along with this scheme to take Hawkes down."

Lily shrugged. "The plan is solid. No reason things shouldn't go as expected."

Storm gave her another telling look. "When it concerns

Hawkes and the Masons, nothing ever works out as expected."

BARRON AND BISHOP DISMOUNTED, saw to their horses, then joined the others in the main ranch house. Ever since Hawkes's henchman had taken refuge on the ranch, they'd upped their vigilance.

"When is Ben due back with the marshal?" Barron asked.

"I expect we'll see them later today," Brody said.

"I don't like that he went alone," Braydon said. "What if he ran into Hawkes and his men?"

"The twins have been keeping an eye on Hawkes's comings and goings," Brody said. "Besides, Ben can take down anyone who gets in his way." The others nodded. Benjamin's skill with firearms knew no equal.

Barron spoke up. "Hawkes has been riding his crew pretty hard around the place. We're not sure if they're looking for Denim or getting things ready for the supposed wedding. They must be aware Denim left on foot, but for all they know, he stole a horse and cleared out of the territory."

"Which is why," Brody said, "we're bringing the marshal here instead of escorting Denim to him. No point taking a chance on running into Hawkes and his thugs along the road."

"Lily has been trying to keep Hawkes distracted with plans for the supposed wedding," Barron added. "When do you expect the phony property deed to be ready?"

"What are you thinking?" Brody asked.

"Thinking that a rough draft for Lily to show Hawkes

might get his juices lathered. He just might let his guard down."

"That's a possibility," Brody said.

At that moment they were interrupted by the arrival of Benjamin and Marshal Philips.

"I understand you have a prisoner for me," Philips said with no preamble or pleasantries. They'd dealt with the man in the past and Barron knew he was strictly business. As professional a lawman as any he'd ever seen.

Brody stood and shook the marshal's hand. "Appreciate you coming all this way."

The marshal cocked his head toward Benjamin. "Your brother was most persuasive. I have to admit, the opportunity to solve the twenty-five-year old disappearance of an entire gang of outlaws is mighty appealing. Where is the snitch?"

"We'll take you to him when the time is right," Brody said. "In the meantime, we're planning the sting to end all stings. We'd like you there when it happens."

Philips raised a brow. "Nobody said anything about a sting. I thought I came here to have a criminal surrender to me after he reveals evidence of a past crime."

"How would you feel about the chance to solve not just a twenty-five-year-old murder, but a few others more recent from around these parts?"

Philips removed his hat and pulled out a chair. "I'm listening. Any coffee in that pot over on the stove?"

"HERE THEY COME NOW," Barron told Benjamin, as Lily's carriage drove into view with Hawkes at the reins and Lily seated next to him. The two men backed out of sight as

Hawkes slowed the rig in front of the Yuma Gentleman's Clothier and Haberdashery.

"I have to hand it to Lily," Benjamin said. "She's one cool cucumber of a lady. Not many folks could spend this much time with Hawkes, pretend to look up to him, and still sleep at night knowing what he's done in his life."

"Lily's something else all right," Barron said. Nothing seemed to ruffle her feathers, unless it was him. Mind you, Lily could get him in a right lather just with a look.

"Place won't be the same once this is over and she's moved on." Benjamin gave Barron a probing look as he spoke.

"Something on your mind?" Barron asked shortly.

"Just making sure you've not got any entanglement with the lady you're pretending to marry. Because that's when the best-laid plans tend to go sideways. There's too much at stake to have anything go wrong next week."

"Why would anything go wrong?"

"Because it usually does. Like now." Benjamin pointed to the street where three men rode up to Hawkes and confronted him as he secured the rig. Lily stood on the sidewalk outside the menswear shop.

"Damn and thunderation!" Barron said, kneeing his horse forward.

Benjamin caught his arm. "What are you doing?"

"What any good fiancée would do. Defending my woman and her companion, as unsavory as he is."

"Be careful," Benjamin said.

Barron didn't respond, but it sure felt good knowing Ben had his back as he rode into the fray. "Hey gents, what's going on?"

"Telling this vermin here he's not welcome in Yuma. Or any place decent folks go."

"Last I checked it was a free country," Barron said mildly, one hand resting on his holster.

"Hey!" one of the others interjected. "You're one of them Mason brothers from Bullet. You hate this murdering bastard more than we do."

"We folks up in Bullet are working on forgiveness," Barron said.

"Not us," said the third man as he pulled out his pistol and waved it threateningly toward Hawkes. Before he could take aim, his weapon was shot clean out of his hand.

The other men's gaze flew toward Barron, who raised both hands showing they were empty.

"See that?" Barron said. "Old Hawkes has a few new friends hereabouts. I'd be careful who you go threatening if I was you."

The three men exchanged a look. "You've not seen the last of us," the ringleader said as he signaled the other two and they rode off.

LILY SMILED PROUDLY as Barron rode up to Hawkes. He looked so handsome astride his horse. She knew how hard it had to be for him to pretend to defend Hawkes.

"Welcome to the family," Barron said, sarcastically.

"Coulda handled things myself," Hawkes blustered.

"Probably," Barron said. "But you didn't need to. This little lady means everything to me, so take good care of her today." He leaned down and kissed Lily's cheek, managing at the same time to slide a key into her reticule without Hawkes noticing. She met his gaze and gave a quick nod.

"I love you, sweetheart," Lily called out as Barron turned and rode back to where Ben waited out of sight. Hearing her words, she gulped. How had the "love" word flown out of her mouth so natural-like?

"Is he always so protective?" Hawkes asked Lily as they entered the store.

"I told you, Barron Mason would do anything for me. And after your fitting, I have a surprise for you."

While Hawkes stood before the large cheval looking glass, modeling the charcoal-hued suit which had been expertly tailored to disguise his girth, Lily pulled out her reticule and peeled off a handful of bills which she passed to the clerk. "Thank you for getting this ready so quickly."

"I'm glad everything is satisfactory, miss."

Hawkes was still in front of the mirror, turning this way and that, admiring himself in his new finery. "I never truly believed in that old saw about 'clothes make the man', but I have to say, I cut rather a dashing figure, don't I?"

"Indeed you do." Lily joined him before the looking glass and, as distasteful as it was, rested her head against his upper arm, the two of them presenting a picture of easy compatibility to the wide-eyed clerk. Lily expected word to travel like wildfire around town and beyond. "Daddy would be so happy to know you'll be at my side on my big day."

Hawkes raised his face to the heavens, as if convening with a higher power. "And in full approval of our partner-ship." He turned back to Lily. "When folks tell me they have a surprise for me, it usually bodes badly."

Lily patted his arm. "Trust me, you'll like this surprise."

He rested one hand on his chest. "Go easy on a gent. Having a Mason welcome me to the family is almost more of a surprise than my old ticker can take in one day."

Lily turned away to hide her smile. Hawkes referring to himself a gentleman meant he was buying this whole charade lock, stock and barrel.

"Can you have the suit wrapped and ready to go when we get back?" she asked the clerk.

"Indeed, miss." The man's face was still a study in shock. "Guy Hawkes is giving you away? And you're wedding a Mason. Did I hear that right?"

"Indeed," Lily said sweetly. "The wedding is taking place on Mr. Hawkes's ranch this upcoming Saturday. Would you and the missus care to join us for the happy occasion?"

"The Masons and Guy Hawkes breaking bread together, not staring at each other down the barrel of a gun? This I have to see."

"I look forward to seeing you there. I've invited a few of the other townsfolk that I've met here during my brief stay as well."

"Will you be moving to the Copper Moon with your husband as all the other brides have done?"

"Of course," Lily said. "After all, it's tradition."

"Did I overhear something regarding a partnership deal in the works?"

"Isn't that lovely?" Lily said with a serene smile. "No more bad blood." She tried not to flinch when the fellow quickly made the sign of the cross, his action raising unhappy reminders of the past.

The clerk met her gaze. "Just saying a quick thanks to the powers above. Most folks around here have been praying for a peaceful resolution to the violence that's been known to seep over here from Bullet."

Lily smiled. "Then Saturday should be a particularly happy occasion."

She turned as she heard Hawkes behind her, back in his normal clothing. "Where to now, little lady?"

"Next stop is the bank."

As their destination was on the next street over, they left the carriage where it was and headed that way.

"I'd be mighty happy to hear you have some more cash waiting for me," Hawkes said.

"Then this will be more than a wonderful surprise. Seeing as it's better than cash."

"Nothing is better than cash," Hawkes said.

Lily cocked her head at him. "Care to make a small wager?"

She was well aware of the sideways glances that came their way on the short walk to the bank. A few of the men cautiously tipped their hats in the direction of her and Hawkes.

Barron was right. Word traveled fast.

She couldn't deny the small tremor of excitement that ran through her at the thought of pretending to be, even for a short while, Mrs. Barron Mason. When had that started? Barron creeping into her thoughts at random moments had been happening more and more frequently.

"Here we are." Hawkes, obviously taking his new role of gentleman seriously, held the bank's door open for Lily to precede him inside.

A clerk rose from behind his desk at their entrance. "The manager is waiting for you, Miss Mayberry. I'll escort you there now."

Lily swallowed her amusement at the way Hawkes puffed out his chest, as if being treated in such a fashion was his rightful due. The only one he was fooling was himself. She reminded herself the further the axe fell, the deeper the wound.

The manager was waiting when they reached the area of the bank housing the safety deposit boxes. "Miss Mayberry." He bowed, straightened and pulled out a heavy keyring. "I was so very sorry to hear of the passing of your dear papa. I am delighted you have chosen to avail yourself of our modest branch and services here in Yuma."

"It's what daddy would have wanted," Lily said. "I believe you are acquainted with Mr. Hawkes."

"Only by reputation," the manager said, coolly.

He didn't offer Hawkes his hand, turning instead to a far wall lined with small numbered doorways. He selected a numbered box and entered his key into the upper keyhole. Lily produced her own key and inserted it into the lower hole. Lily nodded to the man, they turned their keys at the same time, and tumblers clicked. The manager removed the box to a wooden sideboard.

"I will leave you to it," the man said before he retreated. "Please let me know if I can be of any further service."

"Whatcha got in there?" Hawkes stood, literally rubbing his hands together while trying to peer over her shoulder as she opened the lid.

Lily removed a single white envelope, opened it and skimmed the contents before she passed it to Hawkes.

His hand shook as he grabbed it and squinted at the spidery legal jargon, most of which Lily knew to be beyond his reading comprehension. "What's this?"

"The deed to the Copper Moon Ranch, in my name."

Spittle formed in the corner of his mouth. "How'd you get Brody to agree?"

"The how doesn't matter. What matters is that on the day of the nuptials, our solicitor will be on hand to formally transfer ownership to you."

"Ha ha!" Hawkes grabbed her and spun her in a circle, then seemed to realize what he was doing. He dropped her as if his fingers were suddenly burned.

Lily regained her footing and shot him a frosty look.

"You're walking me down the aisle on my wedding day. You're overseeing a mining operation that will honor my father's memory and make us both very wealthy. Please don't presume more than that."

His eyes narrowed. "Wait a minute. If you get even wealthier, it means that Mason cur you're marrying does as well."

"Why should you care? You'll be rich as Croesus and an esteemed member of society." She tilted her head. "Daddy was well-connected with many government officials. I wouldn't be surprised if before long an offer came your way."

"Darn right. I could show them government officials a thing or two."

While Hawkes was distracted with thoughts of future glory, Lily reclaimed the phony deed and returned it to the safety deposit box, which she locked back into place.

"Hey! Why'd you do that?"

"Safekeeping," Lily said sweetly. "We wouldn't want anything to happen to the deed before Saturday, now would we?"

# CHAPTER 11

Lily was getting washed for bed when she heard the sound of footsteps on the front porch. It wouldn't be the first time some amorous buck got the night wrong and showed up looking for female companionship from one of Zara's girls. She flung open the door to send whoever it was on his way, then froze when she recognized Barron.

"Can I come in?" he asked as she stood there, one hand on the doorknob, her jaw hanging open.

"Are you looking for me?"

"Of course I'm looking for you. I stopped by Zara's today in Yuma and asked her where I might find you." He gave a rueful grin. "I have to say this is the last place I would have looked."

"I thought you might be a customer who got his nights mixed up." Lily wanted to ask Barron if he was a regular caller, but some things were better left unsaid.

She let him in and led the way into the front parlor, where she stopped to light a lantern, glad she hadn't gotten around to putting on her nightshirt. She smoothed the pleated front of her silk blouse and hoped it wasn't too wrinkled. He didn't give the place a second look but sprawled across a settee, seeming perfectly at home. She perched on the edge of a dainty upholstered chair and wrapped her arms around her middle.

She hadn't been this nervous around Barron since … since forever. It had been easier when they were hurling insults. She stared down to where the toes of her fancy boots peeked out from beneath her skirt hem. Since she'd called out "I love you" earlier today in a way that felt so natural, it must be true.

Could Barron tell how she felt from looking at her?

She cleared her throat with difficulty. "You didn't say why you were looking for me."

"I wanted to know how it went today with Hawkes at the bank."

Of course he did. Silly to think for one minute that he thought of her all the time, the way she did him.

She steepled her fingers in her lap, proud of how steady she held them.

"It went fine. He totally believed me that the ranch deed will be going into his name right after our nuptials." She couldn't help but blush as she said it. She made it sound as if they were really exchanging vows. "You know, our fake nuptials."

"You've been amazing," Barron said. "The way you strung along Hawkes."

She made a rueful face. "No different from the way I used to placate my pa and tell him exactly what he wanted to hear. That he was the best man to ever walk the earth."

Barron's look grew troubled. "He ever hurt you? Your pa?"

"Not in the way you mean."

Barron's eyes narrowed. "What way then?"

"Just, he was real good at making Rose and I feel worthless. Like nothing we did would ever be good enough. Handed out lots of penance and punishment for imaginary sins against God." She took a breath. "I think belittling us was his way of trying to make himself feel more powerful and manly. Or in his case, God like. He needed an excessive sense of power to lord over others."

"Same as Hawkes," Barron said.

"Exactly like Hawkes."

"You going to go after him one day? Your pa?"

She shook her head. "He used us from the time we were toddlers. His two little blond angels, he called us. We were the magnet to lure folks to come listen to him preach, to believe his self-serving blasphemy. By defying him and leaving, Rose and I took that away from him. Without us, he has nothing."

The whole time she'd been speaking, she felt Barron staring at her lips. Self-consciously she moistened them with the tip of her tongue. His pupils dilated as he watched her. His breathing grew ragged. Lily felt her pulse jump. She leapt to her feet at the same time he did.

"It's getting late. I'd better—" The rest of what she'd been about to say was lost as he pulled her into his arms and kissed her. He felt divine. She melted against him, melted into him, as she kissed him back. Eventually he broke the contact, but kept her wrapped in his arms. She felt his heart racing nearly as fast as hers. She tilted her head to study him, wishing she knew what he was thinking.

"I've been wanting to do that all day. Ever since I saw you in Yuma earlier, so fine and strong and in control." He stared into her eyes. "You called out 'I love you, sweetheart', and I found myself wishing— wishing it was real. That you meant it. But I knew it was all an act."

"That's right," Lily said. "It was all an act. Same as our pretending to be getting married."

Barron released her with seeming reluctance. "It'll be over soon. Things will get back to normal."

"Normal," Lily echoed. She felt suddenly cold without the warmth of Barron's embrace. "I can't wait."

"Me, either."

"I CAN'T BELIEVE this is actually happening," Barron said to no one in particular as he wrestled with his tie, which for some reason refused to cooperate.

Bishop stepped forward and pushed his hands out of the way. "Let me." Deftly his twin fashioned the tie into a proper knot and adjusted it against Barron's shirt collar. He grinned. "You think you're nervous now. Wait till you're really getting hitched. There's a feeling like no other. Elation. Anticipation. Nerves."

"Cold feet?" Barron said, cynically.

"Maybe for some. Shouldn't happen if you know in your heart your intended is the one for you."

"How does anyone know for sure?" Barron asked.

"Don't ask me." Bishop shrugged. "You just do."

"You boys ready?" Brody appeared in the doorway of the upstairs ranch house bedroom. "Ben and Blake have both the wagons hitched. First time ever the ladies have beat you two at getting ready."

"It hardly feels real," Barron told Brody. "This takedown of Hawkes has been a long time coming."

"The time feels more than right," Brody said. He gave Barron a smug smile. "I always knew the two true con artists in the family would come up with the perfect sting."

"You did *not* know that," Barron said. "How could you?"

"Care for a small wager?" Brody asked. "I said as much to Bray that first day when you and Bishop tried to put one over on us."

"We didn't even know about Hawkes then." Barron exchanged a look with Bishop. "Joe was still alive."

"Hawkes's history with this family goes back a long way," Brody said. "I'm just sorry Joe didn't light out of there before it was too late."

"What about all that talk earlier? You weren't happy with how Lily and I got things going."

"I wasn't happy because you two acted on your own. And that's not the way this family operates. We're all in this together, which was apparently a tough lesson for you."

"You took Bishop and I to task more than once over the years, telling us to take things slow."

"The best-laid plans can't be rushed," Brody said. "Not even when it's you two hatching the scheme. Now let's go. We've got our rat cornered and ready to swing."

"And everyone from the marshal's office is in place at Hawkes's as guests?" Bishop said.

"Do you two think for one second any of us would allow our wives and children to set foot near Hawkes's place if we weren't one hundred percent convinced of their safety?"

"Except it's no longer Hawkes's place," Barron said.

"Whoever said 'revenge is sweet' knew of what he spoke," Bishop said.

"Let's not be putting the cart before the horse," Brody said. "Let's just savor the day we destroy Hawkes in front of the entire town, strip him of everything he holds dear and hang him out to dry."

"Before we see him dead," Barron muttered under his breath.

"HAS ANYONE SEE BARRON YET?" Lily asked the Mason clan for the zillionth time that day. She stood just inside Hawkes's ranch house front door with Rose and the other Mason wives. From her vantage point, she could see that most of the guests had arrived and were milling about the area near the pond which had been readied for the pretend ceremony. Her insides were bashing around so hard, you'd think she was saying "I do" for real and committing her life to someone else's.

"Don't you worry," Laura said. "Brody was in charge of making sure Barron gets here on time and in one piece. We're going to go take our places now," she added. She lowered her voice. "Try to relax. Marshal brought men in from all over the territory. Hawkes won't give them the slip."

Rose passed Lily a small bouquet of lilies to carry. Lord only knew how Henrietta managed to have exotic flowers arrive in time for the day, but she clearly had her ways. Their fragrance surpassed all imaginings from years of seeing her name-flower in books. She took a deep, calming breath.

Behind her, she heard the door to Hawkes's den open and then slam. Minutes later Hawkes joined her and Rose, the smell of whiskey overwhelming the delicate fragrance of her bouquet. She clutched the flowers tighter to stop her hands from shaking.

Hawkes gave her a look from beneath beetled brows. "You got the deed, missy?"

"Right here." She indicated a delicate drawstring bag hanging from one wrist. "The transfer will take place at the same time we sign the wedding lines. The solicitor will be there with the minister."

Hawkes let out a satisfied belch that filled the air with more whiskey fumes as he watched the proceedings outside. "Look at all them out there. Never set foot on a real ranch before. Not one this fine."

He cackled and slapped one thigh with a meaty hand. "Who ever thought I'd see this day? All them Masons dancing service. Bowing and scraping."

Lily exchanged a look with her sister. She didn't see any bowing and scraping but let Hawkes have his last little illusion. She touched his sleeve and drew on all her playacting abilities. "It's a truly wonderful day to make everyone's fondest wishes come true. I feel Daddy watching in approval, smiling down on us all."

Hawkes grunted. "I'll be getting the last laugh when I throw the Masons off that ranch and start up the mine."

Lily turned. "You can't throw them off. They live there. I'll be living there as well."

Clearly, Hawkes realized he'd overplayed his hand. "Figure of speech, is all. A friendly reminder who they'll be beholden to for the roof over their heads."

She turned to Hawkes. "That gun in your belt ruins the line of your suit." She pouted. "And you look so distinguished. Please. Today is no day for guns."

She saw him fondle the knife sheathed at his waist. After a long, silent moment, he pulled out his gun and tossed it onto a table in the hall. "I better not regret this."

She flashed a grateful smile. "After today, you'll have everything you ever dreamed of."

A man whom Lily knew to be part of the marshal's contingent poked his head inside. "It's time, miss."

Rose sent Lily a smile. "And you were worried Barron wouldn't make it."

Hawkes gave Rose a rough push. "Get going then. The bride and I'll be right behind you."

Lily counted to six, took a deep breath and tucked her arm through Hawkes's as they started forward. She forced a tremulous smile as heads turned to observe her approach. Most of those watching thought this was real. Did they despise her for being on Hawkes's arm?

She watched Hawkes from the corner of her eye as they wound their way from the ranch house entrance. The guests numbered well over a hundred. Her step faltered. Then she saw Barron. He waited near the edge of the pond with his brothers and the so-called minister, who was really one of the marshal's men.

Their eyes locked. He gave her an approving nod. As his gaze met hers she felt as if they were the only two people here. Everyone else somehow faded into the background.

Her shoulders straightened. Her resolve strengthened. For the first time in her life, people were counting on her. It was a heady feeling, knowing she was responsible for helping end Hawkes's reign of terror.

As Lily and Hawkes reached their places near Barron and the "minister," the background chatter died away. An unnatural silence fell over the area. Lily shifted her weight from foot to foot. Other than the Masons and the lawmen, no one knew what was about to happen.

She exchanged looks with Barron, who stood straight as a soldier, looking handsome and very serious. Her heart gave a tiny hiccup, then lurched someplace down near the bottom of her stomach. What if today wasn't fake? What if the ceremony were real with her and Barron about to make a match?

The idea no longer filled her with dread. Quite the

contrary. She felt a warm glow of comfort. To have someone nearby always. Someone to love and cherish and ....

She blinked herself back to reality.

"Dearly beloved," intoned the fake minister. "We are gathered here today on this joyous occasion to witness the union of this young couple as they embark on the journey of holy matrimony." He cleared his throat and made a big show of flipping a page in his bible. "If anyone here knows of any reason for these two not to be joined in wedlock, let them speak now or forever ..."

"I do!"

The crowd let out a collective gasp. All heads turned toward the rear of the crowd. Marshal Philips strode forward. A dozen men flanked his progress.

Lily was aware of the way Hawkes stiffened at her side. The minister stepped aside as Philips took his place and faced Hawkes. "Sorry to interrupt folks, but this can't wait." He withdrew a sheaf of papers. "By the power given me by the territory of Arizona, I hereby declare this ranch and all other properties formerly held by the person of Guy Hawkes be passed to their rightful owners."

Hawkes's hands balled into fists. His face turned red in anger. "I am the rightful owner."

Brody stepped forward, followed by his six brothers. "I'm afraid that's not exactly true. As of 10 a.m. this morning everything in your name was legally transferred to my brothers and I."

"You can't do that," Hawkes said.

"Already done," Brody said. "These gentlemen are bailiffs. If not for some further developments, they would be here to escort you from the property."

Hawkes puffed out his chest. "Glad to hear there have

been some so-called developments to prevent such a miscarriage of justice."

Marshal Philips turned toward Hawkes. "Actually, I don't think you will be glad to hear what I have to say next. Your former foreman, Mr. Denim, has been kind enough to lead us to a cache of human remains. You're under arrest for the murder of the six gang members who rode with you as Red's Rowdies. I'm confident that the ongoing investigation into the murders of John Jones, Paula Quinn, and Sheriff Yates, with the help of our witness, will implicate you in those crimes as well."

Hawkes pushed Lily hard from behind. She felt a sharp tug on her wrist as she stumbled into Marshal Philips. She caught her footing and looked back to see Hawkes leap into the pond and disappear. Lily covered her ears at the barrage of gunfire from the Masons, the marshal, and his men. Guests screamed and scattered for cover. At the far edge of the pond a stream of bubbles rose to the surface and then stopped.

Half a dozen of the marshal's men leapt into the water and began the search for Hawkes's body.

# CHAPTER 12

A torrent of emotions roared through Lily. She didn't realize how much she was shaking until Barron reached her side.

"Are you okay?" He tilted up her chin and stared deep into her eyes. "You were wonderful."

She glanced over at the pond, where nearly a dozen men splashed their way through from end to end. "Did they get him?"

"Not yet. The pond was deeper than anyone thought. There's talk of dragging the water for his body."

She glanced up into Barron's familiar dark eyes. "Did you and your brothers get what you were hoping for? The long-anticipated take-down in front of everyone?"

"It felt pretty sweet," Barron admitted. "Nothing will bring Joe back. Or make up for all the evil Hawkes has done others through the years. But it's over." He waved an arm. "Look at everyone. They're free from his tyranny." Lily followed his gaze to the gathered crowd, who mingled around, uncertain what to do next.

All through their planning, there had been no talk about what should happen after the takedown.

"Do we tell them the wedding isn't real?" she asked.

Barron's gaze on hers was long and level, impossible to read. She caught her breath. Was he feeling the same as her? Regret. Wishing. Wondering...?

The mood was abruptly shattered as they were joined by Barron's twin.

"It looks like Hawkes gave us the slip," Bishop said.

Lily's eyes flew to Barron. "What? How?" Surely this hadn't all been in vain?

"There was an underwater tunnel leading to the river. He won't get far." Marshal Philips re-holstered his gun as he joined those milling around the pond, peering into its murky depths. "My men and I will make sure of it."

"Let us help," Brody said.

Marshal shook his head. "Best help you can be is deal with the folks here. Keep 'em busy until we've got Hawkes rounded up."

Lily's gaze flew to Barron. "Keep them busy how?"

Barron had that same unreadable look on his face. "I suppose we could get married for real."

"That isn't even funny," she said.

"If you want, I'll announce that the wedding was a ruse to catch Hawkes unawares," Brody said.

"No," Barron said. "Lily and I ought to tell them together."

"Us?" Lily squeaked. "Why us?"

Her heart sped up at the look in his eyes as he met her gaze. Serious. Sincere. Committed.

"Because we started this together. We end it the same way."

*Together!*

Lily swallowed thickly. "Together."

Dizzily, Lily faced the sea of expectant faces that swam before her, grateful when Barron reached for her hand. His clasp was warm. Sure. Comforting. Except it was all fake. Or was it? He didn't have to hold her hand anymore. Folks no longer expected them to act like a betrothed couple.

The crowd grew quiet. Lily glanced over to where the rest of the Mason family formed a united front on one side of the patio. Barron tugged on his tie and cleared his throat a couple of times. Was he as nervous as her?

"So folks!" he said in a loud voice. "Lily and I want to thank you all for coming out today. Sorry to have to tell you there will be no wedding."

A murmur of disappointment rippled through the crowd.

"She jilt you?" a man yelled from the back.

Barron's reassuring smile warmed Lily. He looked younger when he smiled.

"Not exactly, though I wouldn't blame her if that was the case," he said.

Laughter greeted his words and lightened the heavy atmosphere that had befallen the gathering.

"The brothers and I—" Barron waved a hand to where the rest of his family was lined up—"have been working a long time to this end. To destroy Hawkes and everything he holds dear, the same as he has done to us and, I know, to a lot of you over the years. Jail is too good for the man."

He cleared his throat again. "When Lily first arrived, we saw an opportunity for her to help us catch him unawares and set a trap before we placed the final blow. And we wanted everyone here to witness his take-down. To know his reign of terror is truly over. Hence the fake wedding."

"Maybe jail is too good for him," someone else yelled. "Killing ain't."

Barron slid a look toward his family. "We figure time will take care of him in its own way."

"We should strip his house," someone yelled. "After what he done to us."

"Yeah!"

The air rumbled with sounds of agreement. Lily snuck a sideways look at Barron."

"That's not happening here today," Barron said. "Bailiffs have seized the house and property. The law needs to go through the place for evidence of other crimes."

"What's in it for us?"

Lily saw the crowd starting to rally. A group of men banded together and began to move toward the house before Brody and the others stepped forward with her and Barron to face the crowd.

Lily saw Georgina approach Marshal Philips. Moments later the marshal was at their side.

"Miss Georgina has generously offered to have everyone who's so inclined reconvene at the café for a light repast. Shifting folks back to town seems the best move. If Hawkes is still out there, he won't try anything on a large group." He pointed at Brody and Braydon. "How about you Masons start spreading the word and herding people toward their carriages and such?" He waved toward Barron and Lily. "We can have the lovebirds start off the procession."

❧

BARRON OPENED his mouth to refute the "lovebird" term, then snapped it shut. Lily gave him a tremulous smile, and his gut twisted as he remembered she wasn't nearly as tough as she might pretend.

He linked his fingers through hers. "We made a pretty credible happy couple, if I do say so myself. Rose didn't mind you borrowing her dress?"

"She was happy to donate it to the cause," Lily said. She sighed. "I knew Hawkes wouldn't go down so easily. I should have anticipated something like this." When she raised her free wrist, he saw it was marred by angry red marks.

"What happened?"

"He grabbed my bag for the deed. What did he think was going to happen? That he'd somehow wrest control of Copper Moon, despite everything?"

Barron caught her wrist and raised it to his lips to kiss it better. He'd far rather be kissing Lily properly, but this was a close as he dared get. She made a beautiful bride. Just not his bride. He'd spent most of his life fighting. And now he faced the hardest fight of his life. Fighting his feelings for Lily.

She'd been hogtied and repressed her entire life by her bully of a father. He knew she had things she needed and wanted to do. To make the world a better place by ridding it of bullying types. He didn't know how she planned to accomplish it, but he knew he had no right to hold her back.

Hawkes, if he was still alive, wouldn't evade capture for long. Which meant his work here was done as well.

Where would he go next? What would he do? Be strange to be on his own without Bishop by his side. Maybe he could catch up with Percy. Get some ideas as to what he might do now, seeing as running cons and working on the ranch was all he knew.

∼

WITH BRODY and the others in the lead, everyone who'd been at Hawkes's made it back to town with no further incidents. Barron stopped Lily's rig in front of the café, next to a couple dozen other carriages and buggies.

"Would you do me a favor?" Lily asked once they were parked.

"Sure thing. What do you need?"

"Make my excuses to everyone for me."

His gut did an unhappy dive, someplace down around his ankles. "Where are you going?"

"To the house here to pick up my stuff. It's all packed. Then I plan to head to Zara's to return everything she lent me."

He started to ask her where she would go from there, then stopped himself. It was none of his business. "Sure."

"And one more thing?" she asked sweetly.

As if he could refuse her anything. "What's that?"

"Send Rose out so I can say goodbye. If I go inside—"

He understood. Leaving was hard enough without a hundred people tugging at your heart strings, trying to talk you into staying.

AT ZARA'S INSISTENCE, Lily spent the night in the small back bedroom that had been Braydon's when he was a boy. It was hard to imagine the Braydon she knew now had ever been a small child growing up in this house, sleeping in this very small, very short bed. She thought back to her own unhappy, unhealthy upbringing. There were definitely worse places to grow up than this place, surrounded by love.

"Where to now, missy?" Zara asked the next morning as

Lily pulled on her gloves and bonnet and prepared to take her leave.

"Percy very kindly sent Henrietta the name of a family in Colorado Springs who are looking for a nanny to watch their three young children as the family travels back east where they came from."

Zara raised one brow. "You know anything about raising young 'uns? Living in a city?"

Lily shook her head. "I figure, how hard can it be? Sounds like a nice, normal existence. At least for the time being."

Zara barked out a laugh. "I woulda loved to be there when Hawkes got his yesterday." She stirred her coffee. "Course I don't for one second think they'll ever find the vermin. Evil folk like that never get what they have coming."

"He's ruined," Lily said. "Even if he's not badly hurt, where would he go?"

"Snake always has a den," Zara said darkly.

Lily hoped Zara was mistaken.

"I just want to thank you again for your help. I couldn't have pulled this off without you."

Zara gave her a wise and far-seeing look. "It's admirable, this bent of yours to tackle the rotten Hawkeses of the world. Did you ever think there might be a way for you to do that right here in Arizona?"

Lily blew out a breath. "I know it's an impossible goal. I just want to help others have the 'normal' life I didn't."

Zara snorted. "Normal! Ain't no such thing, near as I can tell. Folks just does their best." She cocked her head. "Your problem is you see the world too black and white. You need to adjust your vision. Take in all those different shades of gray."

"What do you mean?"

"You talk about normal. Means different things to different folks. You should stick around a bit. You might be surprised to see what goes on here."

Lily's heart gave a giant flip-flop. Staying put sounded wonderful. Yet she needed to move on. To find her true place in the world.

Zara lumbered to her feet to give Lily a hug. "Learned a long time ago to accept the things I can't change. High time you did the same."

Zara's parting words stayed with her during her walk to the train station. She purchased her ticket to Colorado, hopeful the family Percy knew was still in need of her services, for her meager savings wouldn't stretch far.

As she waited for the train, she took one last look around Yuma. Her gaze snagged on the road to Bullet. Rose had begged her to stay, made her promise to come back.

She was afraid it was one promise she might not keep. How could she bear to come back here, to face all the memories, all the demons of what brought her here in the first place? How could she face Barron, knowing he didn't feel about her the way she did about him?

If she felt lost, it wasn't a new feeling. She'd been lost her entire life, stuck in a world not of her making. This was her chance to create her future. To live her life. One day at a time.

She heard the train's whistle and reached to pick up her valise. At the same time, strong, tanned fingers tangled with hers on the handle. She straightened up.

*Barron!*

"I promised myself I wouldn't do this. Promised myself I'd let you go." He gave his head a rueful shake. "I break a lot of promises, in case you hadn't already figured that out."

Lily's heart beat so rapidly in her chest she could barely swallow. "I don't understand..."

"Me either." He blew out a breath. "Me. You. How I feel. It's this total mish-mash inside of me. Thing is, I feel like you're the only one who can help me unravel it. Figure out what I ought to do next. Which is pretty much anything you want, so long as I get to do it with you."

Lily stared at him. No words formed. Behind them, she was vaguely aware of the train pulling into the station. Of people pushing past as they got on and off the train.

Her own insides were the same mish-mash he had just described. A jumble of fragmented thoughts and emotions and dreams and desires. And as she stared into his eyes, the confusion slowly cleared. Her insides straightened into a nice, soft pillowy cloud of not black, not white, but a nice comfortable gray. A future with room enough for both her and Barron. Because of all her dreams and desires, this man had the most important place in her heart.

"I have no right to do this. To keep you from the train. To keep you from your dream, but that's the way I am: selfish, stubborn. I see my way as the only way—"

Lily placed a finger to his lips to stop the flow of words. "No more making promises you can't keep."

"I promise to love you. To take care of you. To build a good life together, however that looks. And that's one promise I aim to keep."

"That's three promises," she said, teasingly. "You're sure you can keep all three?"

"Cross my heart."

"No more cons and tricks?"

"What you see is what you get. A simple man. One who loves you and needs you more than life itself." He reached for her. "Someone told me once love and hate were near-about the same."

"That must be why I love you. I think I always did. But I tried to pretend otherwise. I didn't really know what love was, let alone what I felt for you, so I pretended to hate you. Yet the entire time, tangled up in those strong emotions, all I was really doing was growing the love I felt first time I laid eyes on you, in the kitchen at Zara's."

He pulled her to him. His arms held her firm, safe, yet with enough love and support to let her be the person she needed to be. The person she was still finding out about. And how much more fun that discovery would be with Barron by her side.

Secure in his embrace, she raised her face, waited for his kiss and welcomed the future. Their future.

*Six weeks later, New Year's Eve...*

POISED at the top of the sweeping staircase in the brand new Grande Hotel, Lily smiled at her sister, Rose, who stood next to her. Rose looked ethereal in a lovely pink bridesmaid gown, carrying a bouquet of pink roses. In a repeat of a few weeks earlier, the entire town of Bullet had once again turned out, this time crowded into the hotel's lobby, spilling into the ballroom and out onto the front steps.

This time was different. This time was for real. And she wasn't even nervous. She was excited to be starting a new year and a new life as Barron's wife. Barron waited below, next to his six brothers, looking up at her with a smile that melted her insides clear down to her toes.

Seated at the fancy grand piano that Henrietta had

imported for the hotel, Amanda gave a nod and began to play the wedding march.

Rose started first down the stairs and a few beats later, Lily followed, one hand gripping her bouquet of lilies, the other hand holding tight to the glossy banister.

She felt like a fairy princess in the dress Storm had fashioned from the smoothest silk and trimmed with French lace at the cuffs and the throat. She reached the foot of the stairs and made her way to Barron's side, happily stepping forward into her new life.

Her friends looked on with happy smiles. Except for Georgina. Georgina didn't look happy at all. In fact, she looked like she was on the verge of tears, as she dabbed at suspiciously shiny eyes with a delicate hankie. Maybe Georgina was one of those women who always cried at weddings.

GEORGINA HEAVED a sigh and tucked her hankie back inside her reticule. She was happy for Lily. More than happy—she was delighted. What made her sad was knowing that this was the last Mason wedding she would be on hand for. No one knew yet of her plans to sell the café and move to Seattle. She didn't want her news to take away from the newlyweds' special day.

In spite of herself, her gaze drifted past the other Mason brothers to Benjamin, as it always did. Georgina had no doubt he would miss her, at least for a short while. But she couldn't pretend any longer. Pretend to be his friend. One who listened raptly to his hopes and fears, his dreams and doubts, his innermost thoughts.

To stay would mean she'd have to pretend she was

happy for him when it came his turn to marry. Pretending to be happy would be impossible. Given that a little piece broke off her heart every time she saw him, knowing he would never look at her the same way Barron was looking at Lily right this minute. It was for the best that she move away. Start over fresh.

Thanks for reading *Barron's Bride*. You might not know how important reader reviews are, but they mean a lot. Just a short sentence saying you enjoyed the book goes a long way with new readers and puts a smile on this author's face.

Review wherever your purchased *Barron's Bride* or on Goodreads or BookBub.

And please keep in touch

Website: KathleenLawless.com
Facebook: facebook.com/kathleenlawlessnovels
Instagram: instagram.com/kathleenflawless
TikTok: tiktok.com/@kathleenflawless

If you haven't already done so, sign up for my VIP Reader's Newsletter and be the first to hear about free books, fan-priced sales, and my new series. http://eepurl.com/bVosbı

Keep reading for a preview of Seven Brides for Seven Brothers, book 7, *Benjamin's Bride*.

Dear Reader

The American West in the last half of the nineteenth century offers my heroines a chance to assert their independence and also introduce them to a hero who is their match in every way. My characters have their own ideas of right and wrong, good versus evil, and deal with it on their terms. It wasn't called the Wild West for nothing. Life was about conquest, survival and persistence,

I love writing a historical genre where the reader, by the simple act of picking up the book, instantly suspends disbelief. She easily forgets about her world and her woes in a tale where no one needs to empty the dishwasher or take out the trash, and adventure lies around every corner.

As an author, it's fun to carry her away to a time and place where anything could, and often did, happen. The customs of the day and the manner of dress might be different from today's world, but people are still people. They laugh, love, hurt and heal. Celebrate and mourn. They live life large. And in the untamed wildness of the settling of the west anything can happen.

Read on for an excerpt from Book 7, *Benjamin's Bride*.

### BENJAMIN'S BRIDE - EXCERPT
Copyright ©2020 Kathleen Lawless

Georgina watched Lily, the latest Mason bride, make her way to the side of her intended. She dabbed the moisture from her eyes, heaved a sigh, and tucked her hankie back into her reticule. She was happy for Lily, delighted that Lily and Barron after a 'pretend wedding' last month, had decided they couldn't live without each other.

Her sadness came from knowing this was the last Mason wedding she would be on hand for. No one knew yet that she planned to sell the café and move to Seattle. She hadn't wanted her news to take away from this special day for the newlyweds.

Her gaze drifted past the other brothers to Benjamin, same as it always did. No doubt he would miss her for a short while. But she couldn't pretend any longer. Pretend to be his friend.

Keeping up the pretense would mean she would also have to pretend she was happy for him when it came his turn came to marry. Pretending to be happy would be impossible—given that a little piece broke off her heart every time she spoke to him knowing he would never look at her the way Barron was looking at Lily right this minute as she reached her side.

Wedding over, Benjamin followed the rest of his family into the hotel lobby. He spotted Georgina in the dining room supervising the laying out of the wedding feast. Marshal Philips stood alongside her chatting her up, and doing a good job of it judging by Georgina's laugh. He'd never heard her laugh like that with anyone other than him.

"You could go join them, you know."

Benjamin stiffened and turned to face Laura, his sister-in-law. "Why would I want to do that?"

Laura just gave him that knowing smile of hers. "I don't know, Ben. Why would you?"

"I don't want to," he said shortly. "Georgina's free to spend time with whomever she chooses."

"Strikes me there have been a lot of times lately when you were her first choice."

"So?"

"Maybe she's tired of being taken for granted," Laura said. "Of being told she's like a sister."

"I don't—" He bit off his words. Hadn't he told her that very thing just a few minutes ago?

"What's wrong with that?" he said. "She has no other family since her ma passed."

"Georgina wants the same thing as most women. A home. A family. Someone to cherish her and make her feel special."

Ben glowered across the room. "Philips seems to be doing a mighty fine job of that right now."

Laura followed his gaze. "It's time someone did."

When Laura wandered over to join her husband, Benjamin headed to the bar for a badly needed beer.

Get your copy of *Benjamin's Bride* today or keep reading to see more books by Kathleen.

## ALSO BY KATHLEEN LAWLESS

Sweet Western Historical Romance
### SEVEN BRIDES FOR SEVEN BROTHERS SERIES

Brody's Bride - Book 1

Bradley's Bride - Book 2

Braydon's Bride - Book 3

Blake's Bride - Book 4

Bishop's Bride - Book 5

Barron's Bride - Book 6

Benjamin's Bride - Book 7

Seven Brides for Seven Brothers Box Set 1 - Prequel & Books 1 to 3

Seven Brides for Seven Brothers Box Set 2 - Books 4 to 7

Sweet Western Historical Romance
### WIDOWS OF THE WILD WEST

Hope

Janie

Sweet Western Historical Romance
### MAIL ORDER BRIDES

Mail Order Olivia

Mail Order Rachel

Mail Order Martina

A Bride for Shane

A Bride for Riley

A Bride for Weston

Mail Order Noelle

Chelsea's Choice

Lila: Rescue Me Mail Order Brides

Here Come the Brides Volume 1

Here Come the Brides Volume 2

**Sweet Contemporary Romance**

Frannie (Always a Bridesmaid)

Baxter (Last Man Standing)

Blue Sky Island

One Cinderella Spring

One Stolen Summer

One Fantasy Fall

One Wondrous Winter

**Sweet Christmas Romance Novellas**

Holly's Wish

No Groom at the Inn

**Steamy Contemporary Romance**
**SECRET SEDUCTIONS**

Her Untamed Cowboy - Book 1

Her Undercover Cowboy - Book 2

Her Unwilling Cowboy - Book 3

Who Needs a Cowboy! - Book 4

Intimate Strangers

**Steamy Historical Romance**

Taboo

Unmasked

Reckless Rogues - Box Set of the 2 Books

**Romantic Suspense**

Final Heat

Afterburn

**Women's Fiction**

Fabulous at Fifty

For a complete book list visit KathleenLawless.com

To be the first to hear about Kathleen's new releases, special fan pricing sales, and also receive a free book, sign up for her VIP Reader Newsletter at http://eepurl.com/bVosbI

## ABOUT THE AUTHOR

USA Today Bestselling Author, Kathleen Lawless, blames a misspent youth watching Rawhide, Maverick and Bonanza for her fascination with cowboys, which doesn't stop her from creating a wide variety of interests and occupations for her many alpha male heroes.

With nearly 50 published novels to her credit, she enjoys pushing the boundaries of traditional romance into historical romance, contemporary romance, romantic suspense and women's fiction.

She makes her home in the Pacific Northwest and loves to hear from her readers.

Sign up for Kathleen's VIP Reader Newsletter to receive updates, special giveaways and fan-priced offers. http://eepurl.com/bVosb1

KathleenLawless.com
Goodreads | BookBub
Facebook | Instagram | TikTok

amazon.com/Kathleen-Lawless/e/B001IXS2SA

goodreads.com/kathleenlawless

bookbub.com/authors/kathleen-lawless

facebook.com/kathleenlawlessnovels

instagram.com/kathleenflawless

tiktok.com/@kathleenflawless